The Sight of Love

By

Kyle Shoop

Other Books by Kyle Shoop

"Senses of Love" Series:

The Sound of Love

The Acea Bishop Trilogy:

Acea and the Animal Kingdom

Acea and the Seven Ancient Wonders

Acea and the Adventure Thru Time

For more information on the author or this series, please visit www.KyleShoop.com

ISBN: 9781711334509

To Carol

TABLE OF CONTENTS

About the "Senses of Love" Series

"Love is the poetry of the senses."

-Honore de Balzac

Love is not only a feeling or an idea, but the result of what is experienced through the five senses.

Touch. Taste. Sound. Smell. Sight.

Through these senses, we may each be touched by love, or express love, differently. This is the purpose of this "Senses of Love" series - to express stories depicting that, although we may each experience or express love differently, it is nevertheless our capacity for love which is unifying.

To that end, the "Senses of Love" series will contain five books - one each addressed to the five senses. This is the second book - the first book, *The Sound of Love*, is already released. The books in this series may be read in any order.

For updates on the availability of each book, please subscribe to my author newsletter by emailing KyleShoop@gmail.com or visit KyleShoop.com

As always, your review on Amazon is greatly appreciated.

Chapter 1

The key is not in the light, it's in the darkness. The shadows. Sometimes it's in the shadows where true beauty is hidden. Indeed, without accurate shadowing, the depth of a painting may not truly be felt, no matter how perfectly the lighting is depicted. It's the dichotomy between light and dark which allows the fullness of the image to be revealed. Ethan recognized this at an unusually young age and, at first, spent much of his time perfecting the shadowing of his paintings.

He began painting young, having learned basic techniques by tracing the outlines of other famous works. He never really stopped to analyze why he was so fiercely drawn into being an artist. As Ethan got older, he'd think about kids who were naturally gifted with the ability to sing, and figured that they were just born knowing that singing was their calling in life. Ethan was a little different though. Looking back, he didn't see himself as being gifted from birth with the ability to paint. And he didn't see painting as his only calling in life. Rather, he just knew that he really wanted to do it. Always. He couldn't remember a time where he wasn't studying other painters, practicing it, or actually painting a commission. He just always wanted to paint.

His parents certainly didn't foster this skill in him, but thinking about his parents was just about the last thing Ethan ever wanted to do. He'd rather have watched an infant draw with mashed up peas instead of think about his parents. At least something compelling might randomly appear from the chaos of smeared peas, whereas his relationship with his parents was the antithesis of compelling.

Though Ethan was always intrigued by visual arts, his desire to actually try painting began at only eight years old. He'd managed to sneak from his parents that he was going to try painting. He'd find copies of famous works and hide them in his room, tracing the outlines when the rest of his family left him alone – which was often. Pretty soon after he started with tracings, he full-on painted rudimentary recreations. It took quite some time, but these recreations peaked with a miniature, but substantially similar, recreation of Vincent van Gogh's The Starry Night. From afar, an amateur wouldn't have noticed the difference between the original painting and Ethan's recreation. By the time he finished it, he was only nine years old. But despite manifesting such a unique talent for mimicking the iconic painting at such a young age, that was the last time Ethan ever did a recreation. This was simply because the painting didn't challenge him enough.

He'd spent months studying the original classic's brush strokes and mixtures of coloring in the paints. He was obviously significantly more advanced in his attention to detail than even teenage painting enthusiasts. But it wasn't Van Gogh's actual painting style which he didn't find challenging enough. Definitely not. He loved that famous painting - everything about it. Rather, it was the fact that he didn't create it himself. As much as he admired several famous paintings, Ethan quickly learned that mirroring another artist's work was just not compelling enough for him.

Still, he learned much from his hands-on study of shadowing in The Starry Night. The shadows in that famous work seemed so simple and overlooked at first. He knew that the average eye would be drawn to the light from the swirling glow of the night sky. But Ethan recognized right away that it was the contrast between those lights and the shadowing of the earth below which allowed the word "beautiful" to accurately convey emotions that were aroused from staring at that great work of art. At only nine, Ethan barely even knew what "beautiful" meant, since he rarely ever heard his parents speak anything close to it. But, still, the first time he saw the painting, "beautiful" was the only word that somehow instinctively came to mind.

And Ethan wanted to arouse that same feeling of beauty in others – only, from his *own* creations.

Unfortunately, the impressionist style depicted from Van Gogh's painting would not be the artistic style he would use to evoke such emotion. Besides learning the importance of shadowing from it, there was one other prominent thing that stood out to Ethan from his tedious recreation of The Starry Night: impressionism was hard to paint!

The impressionist style wasn't one which depicted a realistic, exacting recreation of a scene. Rather, it used a realistic recreation as a baseline, then sought to focus on the emotion of the scene through a subjective approach. This often resulted in blurred, swirling, or large-brushstroke styles. There really wasn't a unified mechanism for drawing an impressionist painting. Rather, if there was a unifying trait, it was to focus on the emotion of a scene instead of how realistic it looked. This often resulted in exaggerated uses of color and style. And this style was just too difficult for Ethan to create. It may have been due to his young age and just starting to cope with emotions, but his intimidation with the style proved a mental hurdle from reattempting to paint an impressionist creation for many years to come.

So eventually, and with the suggestion of a prominent artist whom he lucked into meeting, Ethan switched to a less-prevalent style known simply as romanticism. By the time Ethan was made aware of this style, he was ten years old. So, he was too young to be drawn to the style for any actual romantic aspirations. No, he was drawn into it because of the heightened focus on shadowing which that style more obviously utilized … and because the first painting he'd seen from the romantic era made him think of Robin Hood! As a ten-year-old, Ethan definitely knew who Robin Hood was, and thought any style of painting that seemed to depict that awesome figure was worthy of his time.

The first romantic painting he had run across was at an art gallery in downtown Atlanta. As was his weekly habit, Ethan would follow his father into the city pretending to want to learn his father's profession in neurosurgery. Four days a week, his father would study his cases from his office in their upscale house in the rich suburbs of Atlanta. But once a week, on every Friday, his father would travel into the city to meet with his next patient or to actually perform an expensive brain surgery at the hospital. Ethan reveled in that weekly trip to downtown Atlanta – not because he wanted to learn about his father's profession, but because he utilized the trips as opportunities to study paintings from the local prominent art gallery. The only thing was his parents – and especially his father – didn't know about these self-guided field trips. Just like he hid his recreations and love for painting from his parents, he kept the purpose of traveling with his father to himself.

Each time his father travelled into the city, Ethan tagged along. He'd feign interest in his father's profession during the day, which naturally sparked his father's enthusiasm that his son would follow in his footsteps. His father, Russell Cooley, was a prominent neurosurgeon. Unfortunately, along with this prominence came not only pride, but also an unyielding perspective of practicality. And art – any form of it – is the antithesis of practicality.

This led to deceit by Ethan. Deceit by omission, more specifically. During the morning and later afternoons, Ethan would sit in his father's study at the hospital, pretending to be interested by the dreariness of the scientific culture upon which medicine was practiced. Painting was the only science that existed to the young boy. Ethan waited and waited for the one hour he had each week to study his own passion. The lunch hour.

Right before noon each day, Russell would hand Ethan enough money for Ethan to go buy them both lunch. Luckily for Ethan, his father ate the same thing each day from the same store. And that restaurant was just down the street from Buckhorn Art Company. This is where the deception manifested. Ethan never ate lunch on Fridays, thus unintentionally embodying the phrase "starving artist" from a young age. Instead, he learned that if he ran down to get his father lunch, then he would normally have about forty minutes to stop by the art gallery before needing to be back at his father's office at the end of the lunch hour. By not eating, he earned himself another five minutes or so studying all of the classics, as well as some of the modern paintings, hanging in the nearby gallery.

Buckhorn Art Company was not just an art gallery, it was a school. Due to this, the company owner and well-accomplished local artist, Eugene Turner, kept several halls reserved hanging exact replicas of classical paintings. Eugene charged the public for admission into the gallery. But after a couple of months, he caught onto Ethan's motive. It wasn't Ethan's routine visits which Eugene caught onto first – it was Ethan's pellucid passion for the art.

This passion manifested immediately the first time that Eugene talked to him about the works of art hanging in the halls with the classic paintings. Those halls were not only a timeline of the evolution of painting, but also a visual depiction of the struggles and triumphs of mankind.

From their first conversation together, it struck Eugene as peculiar that the first thing Ethan mentioned was the shadowing of a painting. Never before had Eugene ever had someone point out shadowing as their favorite part of any painting, not even from the self-proclaimed professional artists who frequented the distinguished gallery.

"Are you sure – the shadowing?" Eugene asked Ethan.

"Oh, definitely. Look at it!" Ethan responded, fixated on the well-known work of art in front of them.

"… but it's a can of soup." Eugene was obviously skeptical that anyone could actually find beauty in the shadowing of Andy Warhol's Campbell's Soup Can painting.

Ethan started to explain himself, but Eugene wasn't going to allow it. "Here, follow me." He was going to test the boy.

Eugene took Ethan to observe the painting by Edvard Munch entitled The Scream. It was a famous painting that Ethan had stood in front of several times studying the feelings it evoked. Visually, it reminded Ethan of The Starry Night, so he'd naturally been drawn to this similar work many times before.

"What do you like about this painting, huh? What about it *moves* you?" Eugene intentionally asked the question broadly, trying not to steer the boy towards its shadowing.

"Well, just look at it." Ethan instantly answered, almost as if he'd studied this painting already so much that he was waiting for someone to ask him about it. "It makes the entire painting, doesn't it?" He asked rhetorically out loud. The boy was so captivated by the artwork that he didn't even look at Eugene right next to him.

"What? What makes the painting?" Eugene pressed.

"It's the same thing – the shadowing." There it was. That same answer from such a young boy. Eugene was about to ask for more details about what the boy meant, but he didn't have to. Ethan couldn't withhold his enthusiasm for his perspective of this great work. "I mean – it provides the foundation for the entire painting. It's only because the body of the person screaming is in the shadows that the scream is felt so intensely. It's as though you can hear the scream even though it's really just a painting. Oh, and the shadowing on the dock provides such depth, making the scream feel real."

"Okay, just stop." Eugene interrupted. "Who taught you this?"

"Taught me?" Ethan was confused.

"Boy, have you ever taken an art class before?"

The boy wasn't sure how to answer. He was embarrassed because he hadn't. And he thought that the owner of the great Buckhorn Art Company would think less of him because he lacked an education in the one thing that he wanted so badly.

But the boy didn't have to answer. Ethan's pause of silence and look of embarrassment told Eugene enough.

"What's your name, boy?"

"Ethan Cooley."

"Well, Ethan, my name is …"

But before the man could say his name, Ethan interrupted: "Eugene. I know who you are. I've seen your paintings in here – they're amazing."

Eugene was even more shocked by how Ethan had observed so much about painting in just the short amount of hours he'd been in the gallery throughout the last couple of months. To Eugene, this wasn't just a coincidence. This meant something – something which he couldn't pass up.

Eugene just stared at The Scream for a moment. He wasn't deciding what he should do next, but how he should do it. When a thought came to him, he instructed the boy: "Here, follow me to this one."

They both walked down to a different hall, as if rewinding in time a bit to a different stylistic era.

"Ethan, this one is entitled The Kiss, by Francesco Hayez."

Ethan just stared, intrigued by it. He'd probably seen it before, but only in a passing moment. He'd always favored the impressionist paintings more than the romantic-era paintings like this one. But, upon really noticing this painting for the first time, something very specific about The Kiss stood out to him. In the middle of the painting stood a couple kissing in a stone hallway. The woman wore a blue dress, and the man stood over her, passionately embracing her. Again, though, Ethan was too young to be moved by the romantic passion of the couple.

Instead, he was interested in it for another reason that was obvious to about any boy his age. The man in the painting had a cape and hat on that looked just like Robin Hood.

"Wow, that's so cool …" Ethan said to himself, trailing off in thought as he really studied it for the first time ever. "And look at the shadowing of the couple. It's so realistic and well-done."

"Can you still feel the emotion from the painting just as clear as you can hear the scream in the other one?" Eugene asked.

What Eugene just asked made Ethan pause for a moment. He'd never really considered before that a romantic style painting could depict the same emotion he'd felt from the impressionist paintings. But it did, and he liked it. Even then, there was something even more alluring about this style to Ethan – it would definitely be easier for him to create his own painting in it than the intimidating impressionist style.

"Yes." Ethan said directly.

"Good, I'm glad you like it." Eugene remarked.

"But why are you showing it to me?"

"Because, Ethan, I'm personally going to teach you how to paint like it."

Chapter 2

For as excited as Eugene was to mentor and teach such a uniquely talented, young boy about the fine art of painting, Ethan was even more excited to have received the offer. Ethan's parents rarely gave him any attention, let alone show any interest in what he actually enjoyed. So, he spent much effort concealing his work from them at home. Now, Ethan had found someone whom he could not only talk about his passion with, but whom he greatly respected artistically. He had carefully observed Eugene's own paintings many times prior to actually meeting him. To Ethan, this offer from a prominent artist was the equivalent of winning the lottery.

"Really!?" He blurted out. "That's great! I'll see you next Friday then!"

Ethan began walking to leave the gallery so that he didn't get back to his father late. He had already been cutting things close due to how much time he'd spent staring at the gallery. And that was before Eugene started talking to him about paintings. But Eugene moved quickly to catch up to the boy.

"Wait just a second – hold on." Eugene needed clarification of what the boy was talking about. "Why not tomorrow or Monday?"

"Oh, I can't. My dad only comes to the city once a week on Fridays, and he doesn't know that I come here during lunchtime."

"He doesn't know, huh?"

Ethan just shook his head, not sure if that was a deal breaker for his new mentor.

"Does your mom know?"

"My mom?" Ethan reacted by laughing out loud to himself. "No, she's too busy taking care of the other kids in the house to notice anything that I like."

"And how many siblings do you have?"

Ethan wanted to respond by saying "four too many," but he didn't have time to joke around like he wanted to – he had to get back to his father's office before his father suspected anything awry was going on with his son. So Ethan just simply said, "Four."

"Wow – four, huh?" Eugene eyed Ethan. He still felt strangely and suddenly compelled to pursue teaching the boy everything he knew about painting. So, he didn't want to pass up the opportunity to bring Ethan under his so-called apprenticeship. Perhaps it was because Eugene didn't have any children himself and he found something endearing about the boy. Or perhaps it was because all of his other students were older than Ethan, and were only learning to paint out of educational aspirations rather than an innate desire for the ancient art. Eugene only spoke briefly with Ethan, but he could see it. He'd been around enough students to know passion and talent when he saw it. And that was rare.

Eugene threw up his arms, willing to take Ethan on as an apprentice on whatever terms the boy's circumstances permitted. "Fridays at noon it is, then. I guess that's enough time, anyways – since it is free." Eugene would have it no other way than to be free. True interest in art shouldn't be restrained by monetary ability. Besides, if the lessons led to a true, lifelong passion in the boy, as Eugene hoped it would, then it may just pay itself off in the long run.

Ethan's eyes lit up when he heard the word "free."

"Free?!" He repeated in excitement.

"Yes – free. Does that work for you?" Eugene quipped, trying to make a joke.

"Oh boy, does it! Now I can finally buy lunch instead of

spending that money to come in here."

Those were the last words the young boy said before he turned and ran out the door, back to his father's hospital. But those words confirmed Eugene's desire to teach the boy. When he had made the offer to teach him, Eugene didn't even know of the boy's sacrifice to starve himself just to stare at the paintings. This impressed Eugene to no end.

The weeks turned into months, and the months changed into years. Each week, Ethan was religiously on time and soaked up Eugene's mentorship to no end. The days in between lessons were never ending moments of torture for Ethan as he wanted nothing more than to learn and practice the craft.

In addition, Ethan no longer had to hide his main painting supplies in his room. Eugene not only gifted him with painting supplies, but also gave Ethan space to stash his paintings. And when Ethan turned sixteen years old, Eugene surprised him with his own room inside of the gallery that he could use as his own studio. Ethan was shocked and thankful beyond words. He would frequently find reasons to tell his parents why he needed to travel into the city. But really, he was just using it as a ruse to go to his studio. And eventually, his parents even stopped asking where he was, leaving him wondering if they even realized that he was gone for several hours after school most days.

Still, Ethan's parents never caught on to his weekly lessons from Atlanta's most prominent artist and painting-connoisseur. Ethan never felt bad about concealing his passion from his parents. He didn't even consider it a lie. This was because Ethan could never actually remember a time where either of his parents asked him what he enjoyed doing. His father was keen on his eldest son following in his footsteps into neurosurgery. His mother remained preoccupied with the other, younger children, relying naively on her eldest son being independent.

Over the years, and certainly into his teenage years, this lack of emotion from his family only left Ethan feeling empty and truly alone. Eugene was really the only person who not only shared his interest, but also was willing to listen to Ethan's perspective on art.

"Ethan," Eugene told him on his nineteenth birthday, "You are not only my best student I've ever had, but I consider you my equal." Eugene was standing at the doorway to Ethan's studio, staring at all of the canvases hung around the room which contained Ethan's romantic-style paintings.

"I …" Ethan said, turning to Eugene and not knowing how to even respond to such an unexpected and genuine compliment. In all of the years which Ethan had studied from Eugene, he never even hoped to be considered his equal. Ethan had always seen the opportunity with Eugene as an opportunity to learn from the singular, living artist who he put on a pedestal. He was always nothing more than appreciative of Eugene's graciousness toward him.

"No, I mean it." Eugene interrupted, not even allowing Ethan to say thank you. "Look at your work, Ethan – it's *beautiful.*"

Eugene's continued compliments struck Ethan. Ethan was always so engrossed in what he felt compelled to express that he'd never really taken a moment to step back from his own creations and see what others might feel from them. He looked around the studio, staring at about twenty or so of his most recent romantic works.

"And so I think it's time that you hang them in the gallery for others to appreciate."

"Really?" Eugene's compliments had left Ethan stunned, but this offer was even more shocking to him. Ethan got up from his easel in shock. Never before had he expected, let alone hoped, that he would one day get to hang his own work in the galleries of the great Buckhorn Art Company. He'd stared countless hours at paintings selected to hang on those gallery walls, and knew just how high Eugene's standards were when selecting modern art for them. "Eugene, that's the best birthday present ever! Thank you so much!"

The excitement shown in Ethan's face resonated just as loud as the scream in the famous impressionist painting that the two bonded over years ago. But if Eugene's offer was shocking to Ethan, then he was left completely speechless by the next things Eugene said.

"Oh, that isn't my birthday present. This is." Eugene walked over and handed Ethan an envelope."

"What is this?" Ethan asked, dumbfounded.

"I have no children or spouse, Ethan. And I'm getting up there in age."

Ethan listened intently, not sure what was going on. He shifted his glance from Eugene to the envelope and opened it up.

"It's my will, Ethan. I'm leaving it all to you."

Ethan didn't know how to react. As the years had drifted by, Ethan no longer considered Eugene just his distinguished mentor. Eventually, Eugene turned into his confidant. And after that, Ethan truly felt that Eugene was really the only father figure in his life. Now, Ethan was learning that Eugene felt the same way. Ethan wished he could draw what he was feeling because words were not always his strength. At this moment, he couldn't think of anything else to say but "thank you."

"No, thank *you*," Eugene emphasized before embracing his long-time friend, and the first living painter whose works had ever genuinely moved him.

Chapter 3

In only a couple short months, Eugene's health had deteriorated significantly. It was as if he'd foreseen this happening and his present to Ethan was not happenstance. There was nothing in the world more painful to Ethan than watching his father-figure physically unable to care for the gallery as he once did. Eugene would shuffle slowly up and down the hallways despite Ethan's admonitions to get some rest. Long ago, Eugene stopped teaching his painting classes, handing them off to Ethan's instruction instead. It was bittersweet to say the least.

But Ethan would never forget the moment when it all changed. He was in the middle of hanging a newly-received replica of Frida Kahlo's famous self-portrait when it happened. Ethan jumped at the sound of a loud thump which came from the front of the store. It was a loud, thunderous sound that Ethan knew could only be made from a person collapsing onto the gallery's wooden floor. Ethan ran to Eugene's side, but it was too late.

The next several days were a blur. Paramedics. A funeral.
Reading the will at an attorney's office. Ethan's world was
instantly changed. He should have been elated to have inherited
such a distinguished estate. Even the local art community was
experiencing the dueling emotions over the loss of Eugene, but
thrill that the legacy had been preserved in Ethan's more-than-
qualified hands. However, none of it mattered much to Ethan.
He was still overcome by the loss of Eugene. That hole which
existed so long ago due to his family's emotional absence in his
life had been filled by his mentor. Now, Eugene was gone. That
hole was torn even wider agape.

On his first real evening alone in his new business, Ethan
just sat on a stool in the middle of a hallway staring at Eugene's
paintings. A deep sea of emotions flowed through Ethan's
entire body, and he couldn't contain them. Tear after tear fell
while his gaze penetrated into the soul of Eugene's works.
Ethan hoped that somehow, if he was able to feel Eugene again
through his works, then maybe his presence would live on in
the gallery. He didn't know if something like that could really
happen, but his sense of loss was so great that he wished
desperately to fill the void in any way.

Then it came to him. An idea. It was as if a veil was lifted from his mind when the idea struck. He needed to let Eugene go in peace. He needed to stop thinking about his own desires, and instead think about how this was a natural part of life. And to do this, he was going to have one final celebration of Eugene's life through an evening where the entire public could come appreciate the gallery for free. He would display all of Eugene's paintings in one final memorial of his life before moving on. But even more than that, for one night, Ethan would give to the entire public what Eugene had provided him - the ability to come into the gallery to appreciate true art unrestrained by monetary ability. There would be food, simple music, and welcoming to people from all walks of life. Anyone who held even a spark of interest in art would be welcome. It was a beautiful idea.

The evening came, and Ethan enlisted the help of his art students to throw the event. They were so excited at paying tribute to their long-time instructor that they pretty much took over planning the event. They completely ran with the idea and did all of the marketing and executing of it. They even each prepared countless hors d'oeuvres and refreshments just in case the attendance was as they'd hoped. The evening was to be one to memorialize Eugene with the dignified respect which they each held for him.

That evening, the students and Ethan all came dressed up for a black-tie event, despite being willing to welcome anyone from off the streets into the gallery. And much to their excitement, the event was extremely well received. It was quickly apparent that the public not only supported the gallery and its cultural benefit to downtown Atlanta, but that Eugene was highly regarded throughout the community. Indeed, Ethan personally welcomed several attendees who traveled from all over the county just to honor Eugene's life.

An interesting range of emotions were exhibited by the diverse crowd. Those who knew or had met Eugene were no doubt solemn. Many others attended to express their appreciation to Ethan for his plan to continue on with the Buckhorn Art Company. And there were even more people who stopped by to utilize the free admission into the gallery. Ethan especially welcomed those newcomers, in keeping with the spirit of Eugene's passion and goal to have the arts be accessible to all.

The halls on which the replicas of the classic paintings hung were undoubtedly popular. Besides those halls, Eugene's paintings were also understandably well-observed. This warmed

Ethan, as his sole purpose for the night was to seek to move on from losing his friend. Seeing the popularity and appreciation of Eugene's work provided relief to Ethan beyond words. Many individuals and families gathered around his work to not only pay tribute, but to really study what Eugene had wanted to express.

However, there was one couple that Ethan saw staring at Eugene's work who he did not welcome. His parents. Their attendance was extremely surprising to Ethan, and at first, he didn't know how to react. He didn't even know if they knew that their own son was putting on the event. Surely, they didn't. Nothing had ever been said to them about the gallery, Eugene, or even painting. But, then, why would they be here? They never showed any interest in painting or art.

Ethan's mind scrambled about why they would be here. Perhaps it was the free admission and the gallery being just down the block from his father's hospital which led to their attendance. When he realized that it was Friday night, his regret at so carelessly putting this on during the one day his father was in town quickly set in. That had to be it. Free admission, and now his lifestyle was blown.

Ethan's mind next went to what he needed to do about

this dire situation. Should he hide in his own studio-room and wait for his parents to leave? No. He was not missing out on Eugene's night on account of his parents. So, he made up his mind and knew what he would do.

Ethan walked straight over to his father and mother, who stood near the entrance of the building observing one of Eugene's artworks.

When his mother turned and saw him, her face lit up. "Oh, Ethan, hi!" She said, smiling at him. She had dressed up for the occasion, which now told him that they had planned this evening out. She never had time to dress up nice due to being so overburdened with the younger siblings. Seeing this pained Ethan, because he knew he was about to ruin their special evening out. As he approached closer to them, his mother continued: "So this is where you…"

But Ethan didn't let her finish, interrupting them. "Mother. Father. I need to tell you something." He said sternly. Ripping the band-aid off quickly was the only way he could handle this tough conversation. He was never this stern and cold toward them at home. Never. But what he needed to tell them was so difficult that the only way he knew how to say it was to get it over and done with.

His father cocked his head at the unusual tone in Ethan's voice, listening intently. Ethan could see that his father's eyes were bloodshot from after a long day of concentrating at the hospital. This also told Ethan that they had sacrificed to come to this free art show. That would also make it hard for Ethan to ruin their night with his decision.

"I'm not coming home."

Though his father's eyes were already blood-shot, there was still an immediate, stark change in them which looked pained at Ethan's response.

His mother looked to his father, unsure of how they should react, before looking back at her son sadly. "You mean … never?" All three of them knew what he meant, but she had to try and confirm it just out of the dread of now losing one of her kids from under her roof.

"That's right, mother. I don't need to."

"But what about all of your stuff back home? Surely you want to come get that, right? Or, we can still keep a room for you there if you ever change your mind and want to come back…" Her hopes were in vain, and they all knew it.

Ethan shook his head. "Everything I need – everything I've ever needed – is here." Those words stung, as sincere as

Ethan meant them. He didn't want to be backbiting or unloving to his parents, it was just the honest truth to him. Still, he tried to soften the sudden blow to his parents by explaining himself. "The prior owner, Eugene, left it all to me. And I'm nineteen now. Most kids my age are off at college anyway. So, you'll do fine without me. This is my home now."

One thing stood out to Ethan about the news he just delivered to his parents – neither of them looked surprised that he now owned the great Buckhorn Art Company. They didn't even ask him any questions about it, either. This made his father's response all the more cryptic to him, leaving Ethan wondering what exactly was meant by it.

His father placed his hand on his shoulder and spoke calmly. "We always knew this day would come."

Ethan wanted to ask his father what was meant by that – whether he meant that the day would come where he moved out, or whether they somehow knew about his work at the gallery. And in the years that would follow, not asking his father for clarification would become one of his largest regrets. But in that moment, a stronger emotion left Ethan speechless. It was the feeling that he was letting his father down. All of those years giving his father false hope had now accumulated and

Ethan realized for the first time just how damaging his actions were. He felt embarrassed for leading his father on the whole time. Ethan didn't regret following his own passion, but he deeply regretted lying about it. It was in this moment that Ethan wished he was as good with words as he was with painting feelings because he couldn't find a single word to say – even "sorry."

His father caught on. His hand still on Ethan's shoulder, he drew his son in. During the embrace, his father simply said, "You will do great at this. I know it."

The understanding tone in his father's voice surprised Ethan. When his father let go, he looked to his mother. A tear slid down her cheek, which surprised Ethan. It left him wondering if he had somehow misinterpreted her lack of interest in him as her really giving him space to do what he was drawn to. This thought lingered with him while he also hugged his mom. When it ended, he tried to temper his prior sternness with an invitation.

"If you ever need me, this is where I'll be." The words had already come out, and Ethan was worried that it sounded distant – that he again didn't express himself as he really felt. He wished he had a paintbrush and canvas in front of him to paint his parents a picture of how he felt. He'd paint a giant wave of an ocean engulfing his tiny self in its tempest. That was how he felt in this moment. But instead, his weakness for words had left his parents in tears of dismay.

His father managed a smile. "Could we stay here until we're done? You know how rare a night out is for us, and there's still so much more your mother would like to see."

Yet again, his parents' response surprised him. Never before had Ethan seen any hint of an interest from his parents toward art, and yet here they were wanting to spend a rare night out in an art gallery. Perhaps this was an olive branch being extended by them to Ethan, now that they knew of his passion for paintings. And it was a branch he was willing to welcome.

"You're always welcome here." He paused for a moment and looked at them both. He knew that this was goodbye, he just didn't know how long it was goodbye for. He'd hoped that the next time he saw them was in his gallery, since he had invited them to return whenever they needed him. "Goodbye," was all he said next, choosing to be done ripping the band-aide off.

With that, he turned around to get lost into the raging sea of emotion which his home of artwork had so long fostered.

He was familiar with its endlessly enveloping arms. And it was his new home. Just as he needed to move on from Eugene, he knew that he now also needed to find a way to fill the void of his parents – no matter the size of that void.

He turned to focus on the ocean of other guests, but something unusual caught Ethan's eye.

On this free night open to the public, patrons were mostly only stopping to stare at the classic works of art and Eugene's paintings. As to the other modern works, even his own, they all just passed by without giving them much thought. Except one person. Out of the corner of his eye, the deeply bright red hue of a woman's hair burned as unusual. So, he turned and observed her, just as if he was observing a painting. Only this time, he was studying her at a distance from the other end of a hall.

The actions between her and everyone else was so strikingly different that he knew he just had to approach her. She had stopped and actually was staring at a painting in the modern hall. Ethan couldn't tell which painting she was studying, but it didn't matter. He could tell she was being drawn into one, and that stood out as vastly different from all the other guests who had just casually passed by that hallway. It was as if she had planted her roots in the hallway to study a painting, while everyone else breezed by in the wind.

After a few moments, Ethan began walking casually toward the woman. She had undoubtedly not noticed him, since she was still fixated on a painting. As he got closer, her image became clearer. The color of her red hair intensified, and he saw that she was probably just a couple years older than him. And the painting she was staring at wasn't just any modern painting – it was one of his.

"What do you think of it?" He asked, startling her from behind.

"What do you think the artist was trying to say with it?" She just asked back. Her question was surprising to Ethan. He'd asked hundreds of people over the years what they thought of paintings, and not once before had he been asked a question back, let alone about the artist's intent.

She turned and looked at Ethan, and once seeing him, she broke out in a wide smile. Her red hair contrasted with her bright green eyes. In this completely unexpected moment, Ethan instantly knew he had just met the most beautiful woman he would ever set eyes on.

The fact she smiled when she saw him either said that she

liked him back, or that she knew him already. But Ethan didn't have a clue who she was, so he just wanted to see if he was missing something.

"I'm sorry ... do I know you?" He asked.

"I don't know, do you?" She said back, still smiling while trying to give him a hard time.

"No ... I don't think I do, at least."

"Well, then," she said while extending her hand, offering for him to shake it. The look in her eye and tone in her voice had a hint of excitement in it that made Ethan think she was smiling for the first reason – she was caught off guard, just like he was, at their sudden meeting. She liked him back; he could see it in her eyes. "I'm Rose."

Chapter 4

Rose. Rose Abernathy. Such a beautiful name for such a beautiful woman. And her name was fitting too, as the initial sight of her bright red hair being fixed among the other patrons who passed by stood firm like a rose in wind. Rose was going to change Ethan's life. He could just feel it.

Ethan wanted to blurt his name out in return as he reached to shake her hand. But even though he was immensely intrigued by this unexpected encounter, he still had to focus. Not only was he drawn into the sight of Rose, but he was intrigued by how intently she had been studying one of his paintings.

He didn't know if Rose knew that he was the painter. Part of him hoped that she did – that she was using her fascination with it as a means to impress him. This would confirm his inclination that she was attracted to him just as he was instantly, and breathtakingly, captivated at the first sight of her. But the other part of Ethan hoped that she didn't know it was his painting. This way he'd know that she was genuinely studying the painting for what it was conveying. This would confirm her objective interest in it.

Ethan wanted to test this out. Because of this, he caught himself in the split moment before he said his name, choosing to not yet divulge it.

Instead, he stood there holding her hand as he shook it, looking her in the eyes. She stared straight back at him, waiting for what he would say next. The moment lingered a little longer than it should have as Ethan searched for what he should say next. His mind stumbled as he stared into her eyes, becoming visually distracted at the deep green hue of her eyes. The longer he stared, he wondered if he could ever paint such an intricate mixture of colors, as the interior of her iris turned slightly golden closer to the pupil. The contrast of this deep coloring to her red hair was striking. He felt strangely compelled to try to capture her beauty in a painting.

But he needed to say something … soon.

"Well …" he murmured, "… what do you think?"

"Of what?" Rose asked vaguely while still staring Ethan right in the eyes. A playful smirk adorned an edge of her lips, signaling that she was not just talking about the painting any longer. "I think it's breathtaking, and I could stare all day."

But then Rose turned to the painting, staring at it again. Ethan was enchanted. He'd met many women before who seemed to use his art as a way to hit on him. He used to fall for it sometimes, too. No man's ego is impenetrable to compliments. But Rose was vastly different from the prior advances.

It was in her eyes. He could see it easily as she stood and stared at his painting. The moment she turned to reexamine the work, it was as if she was no longer trying to impress him. Irony would have it that her objective fixation on the art actually resulted in Ethan becoming even more drawn to Rose.

Ethan turned and looked at his painting. He remembered each brush stroke, each paint mixture, and each decision he'd made while painting it. He'd entitled the piece 'Embrace the Light.' It was a painting of a couple sitting on a sandy beach, with the man's right hand wrapped around the woman's back. Their backs were turned to the audience as they sat and stared at the serene sun hanging in the sky just above the woman's head. The light emanating from the sun illuminated the woman more than the man as they sat and embraced while basking in the warmth of the light.

"You know," Rose said to break the silence. "You don't

have to like the painting to impress me."

Ethan chuckled. He loved her playful banter, and loved her statement even more. This told him that she didn't know it was his painting. And that meant Rose was objectively drawn into his painting, which intrigued him even more than he otherwise would have been.

"What makes you think I'm trying to impress you?" He asked. But before Rose could come up with a quick retort, Ethan continued: "Maybe *you're* trying to impress *me*."

Rose turned her head briefly and smiled as Ethan stood next to her staring at his painting. Her motion was quick, but he caught onto it. Her tone became even more excited and accepting of Ethan's challenging response.

"Ok, Mr. Anonymous." Rose now turned all the way to look at him directly again. The shimmer in her eye intensified. "Would you like me to impress you?"

Ethan now shifted away from his painting and was smirking in response. "Think you can?"

"Challenge accepted." She said. She was about to return to staring at his painting, but Ethan quickly interjected.

"Let's have some fun – what do you say?"

Rose raised a single eyebrow, intrigued by the idea of the

sudden game between the two strangers.

"If you impress me more, then I'll tell you my name."
Ethan said. Rose cocked her head, listening closely as Ethan
continued his proposal for the game. "And if I impress you
more, then I get to see you again."

"Really?" She pressed. "Now, that doesn't sound like I'm
going to lose either way." Bingo. Ethan's suspicion was
confirmed. She was into him, though he doubted that there was
any way for her to be drawn into him more than he was
instantly drawn into her. And with what he had planned, he was
going to get to see her again.

"Deal?" He asked, reaching his hand out to shake hers
again. It was really just a ploy to be able to touch her again – to
feel the way that the softness of her skin was like delicate brush
strokes which he wanted so badly to run off and try to emulate.

"Deal!" She practically yelled out while shaking his hand.
She quickly ducked her head down in embarrassment, though,
when she realized how loud her excitement had come out. She
giggled for a brief moment, before turning to inspect the
painting. The moment that she did, her seriousness returned.

She began describing what she saw in the painting to
Ethan. But even though she had turned back to look at it,

Ethan stayed near her staring at her eyes instead. He didn't need to see the painting, he already had it memorized. He instead wanted to memorize the new work of art he just met.

"The artist is being coy, isn't he?" Rose described first.

"How so?"

"Well, just look at the title – 'Embrace the Light. The way it's painted would make you think that it should really be titled 'Embrace *in* the Light' – because the man is holding the woman while they watch the sun. But it's not. So, this would leave someone thinking that the couple is embracing the light from the sun. But not to me. Notice how the sun is positioned just perfectly over the woman so that she is illuminated. *She* is the light. And the man is embracing her. Beautiful idea to paint, right?"

Ethan was deeply complimented from Rose's interpretation. But he still stared at Rose's beauty while he stood watching her study his work. The moment of silence told him he should say something, but before he could, Rose continued.

"But that's not even it. The biggest question of all is whether it's a sunrise or a sunset that the couple is staring at. There's no discernable hint. You can't see the age of the couple

39

to know. And you can't tell what time it is in the painting. So, you're left wondering if the light is the beauty that comes from the beginning spark of a relationship, or instead from the beauty that's manifested from years of devotion. Or, maybe, that's the point of the whole painting – maybe, the artist wants to convey that there's beauty in the differing light that comes from all stages of a relationship."

Rose exhaled to take a final moment and think on the subject before turning to Ethan.

"Do I win?" She asked, now trying to resume being light and cheerful for him. But Ethan wasn't going to let her shift away from how much enjoyment she actually got from her interpretation of his painting. Just as Eugene had wanted to foster his innate passion for art so many years ago, Ethan now wanted Rose to know that it was okay to be passionate about how she was moved by art. She didn't need to throw that aside to try and impress him with her natural lightheartedness and excitable energy.

"Well, I'm definitely impressed by your interpretation of it. But does it *move* you?" Ethan asked simply. He wanted to stare back into her eyes, but instead turned to look at the painting, signaling that he took her impression of it seriously.

"Does it move me? I mean – how could it *not*?" The absurdity of the question almost angered Rose. She again ducked her head down from among the other patrons when she found herself speaking too loud again in the gallery.

"How?" Ethan asked – curious at what her response would be.

"The painting is beautiful, don't get me wrong. The style, the details, all of it. But what's even more beautiful is the emotion it conveys. If you're wondering what emotion it evokes in me – I can't answer that!"

"Why not?"

This time, Rose's exhale wasn't out of appreciation of the painting, but out of the difficulty she was having in explaining her emotions in words. "You see – it's like the palette of color which the artist …" Rose paused while looking up at the title nameplate, "… Mr. Ethan Cooley … used when painting it. Did he use just yellow for the light? No, of course not. He had a full palette of colors to use. In the same way, it evokes a full palette of emotions in me. Even the shadowing used on the couple – the intricate, perfectly balanced shadowing – has a purpose. And from it I get a sense of serenity, love, warmth, and … well, many more things."

The Sight of Love

There it was. That single word and single thought told Ethan instantly that Rose was the only girl he would ever need in the world. That she was the only source of light he wanted to embrace during a sunrise or sunset. The fact that she not only was beyond beauty in sight but also in thought enchanted Ethan. Before today, he only believed in love at first sight when referring to a painting. But now, love at first sight held a much deeper meaning to him. She was more beautiful than any painting he could ever hope to paint. She didn't know it yet, but she'd won him over – in all ways. She'd also won their game. But now it was his turn to try and impress her. He could never actually impress her more than she just impressed him, but he held the upper hand in making her at least think he won the contest.

"Okay, now your turn." Rose's look was surprisingly one of desperation. Ethan interpreted it as a look of desire – not just for him, but in desiring that her zealous passion for the painting would be accepted.

Ethan and Rose were now standing just a foot away from each other. The other patrons just swirled meaninglessly around them as they stared into each other's eyes. A moment ago, they were two strangers in the sea of people attending the art gallery's popular event. Now Ethan was interpreting Rose's look as not only desire, but as an invitation. Ethan reached out and delicately wrapped one of his arms around Rose's waist as they both turned and looked again at the painting. When she didn't flinch, he knew their passion had become ignited. Ethan was relieved, because he had not yet even shown his upper hand to win the contest and see Rose again.

"Rose, I'm Ethan Cooley."

Rose smiled and jostled her head in surprise – instantly turning to stare straight back into his eyes. "You are?" She then shifted her eyes to look back at Ethan's painting. She glanced at it for just a second before looking again into Ethan's eyes. She squinted as she studied his eyes, wondering if the depth of the painting was mirrored in the depth of his eyes. When she quickly saw it, her excitement burst out as though it could not be contained any longer. The well of desire that Ethan's painting had summoned in her now was funneled into a desire for the man who held her.

Ethan suddenly saw a spark ignite in Rose's demeanor. She leaned in and kissed him on the cheek. Though the moment between when he got the courage to touch Rose and when she kissed him was really only a few seconds, it felt like all time had paused for Ethan. No longer did he see any other people walking around them in the gallery. No longer was he concerned with having broken off from his parents just moments earlier. No longer was he reeling in sadness from losing Eugene. He'd met her. The one. She was Rose, both in name and in looks.

Ethan didn't even have to say anything back to Rose after she questioned that he was the painter. She'd studied him. She knew.

"You are!" She exclaimed. Though Rose could have been embarrassed about interpreting Ethan's painting to him without knowing he was the painter, Rose's exhilaration that followed was quite the contrary. "Well, you definitely win, then! Your painting impressed me – as you can tell."

"Let's call it a draw," Ethan offered.

Words didn't matter anymore between the two. The competition didn't matter. What mattered was only that they'd been brought together by a passion, and they both knew it.

"Draw." Rose agreed simply. "… but I do kinda feel like you cheated."

"What? Cheated? Me? No…." Ethan enjoyed the break that Rose brought him with her playful tone. It was rare that he got to feel so flirtatiously at ease with someone, as his romantic-style painting naturally required stoic seriousness.

"I mean, you did kinda cheat…"

"How?" Ethan played naive.

But Rose didn't keep playing along. She just couldn't hold it in any longer as she stood there looking into Ethan's endlessly deep eyes while he held her waist. Those eyes were more intricate than the painting that evoked so much emotion in her. She leaned forward again. She had to. Just as shaking his hand was a ruse to feel him, she needed to feel him again. This time, she kissed him on the lips.

Ethan could read Rose, just as she had read his painting perfectly. He also could not hold it in any longer. As soon as she moved her lips toward his, he reciprocated – unbridling the passion he'd felt for her the first moment he saw her standing down the hallway.

If ever a kiss was meant to last a lifetime, Ethan and Rose's was meant to transcend time.

Rose pulled away slowly and leaned her forehead on Ethan's. "So I'll see you again then?"

"Absolutely." He said.

"Tomorrow night?"

"Wanna come back here to my gallery?"

But Rose's response surprised Ethan. She pulled away from him slightly and looked around at all of the other walls containing centuries of artwork. Then she shook her head. "No."

"No?"

Just as Rose had read his painting perfectly, she was now reading him the same way. "Ethan, when was the last time you really left the art gallery?"

Her question gave Ethan pause. "I don't know – a couple days ago for Eugene's funeral, I suppose."

She quickly interjected. "No, I mean like *really* leave the gallery. Not just physically. You know – up here." She then tapped on the side of Ethan's head.

Ethan kinda smirked. Rose's lighthearted, quirky personality was a breath of fresh air which he immediately knew would balance out his overly-serious tone.

"Um ... never?" Ethan was now full-on smiling, being sarcastic back at her. He knew where this was leading, so he was willing to play along.

"Okay, then. Tomorrow night. 7pm. I'll meet you at Sweet Shack Café. Okay?" Rose proposed.

Rose could have said anything and Ethan would have agreed. He was absolutely absorbed by everything about her. "It's a date."

Chapter 5

The date was not until the next evening, and the time until then felt like a world away. Rose had kissed him on the cheek one more time before she danced off into the night.

Ethan's mind swirled and his emotions were bursting at the seams. He feigned interest in the remaining patrons that night until they had all left him alone in the emptiness of his gallery that he now owned alone. But he wasn't alone. Passion and desire were his new companions – enflamed by having met the most beautiful woman he knew he could ever meet. On a night which he had assumed would end in despair and loneliness, love had allowed him to cast those feelings aside like nothing more than an afterthought.

The gallery needed cleaned up, but he didn't care. He had more pressing priorities. Only one thing was on his mind. That one thing was his only priority this evening. He had to paint.

Ethan walked back to his studio and removed a new blank canvas. Instead of putting it on his desk, he hung it against the wall. The large white canvas in front of him was a world of possibility. For the first time since he was young and recreated The Starry Night, he felt inspired by the endless potential for art. At such a young age, he had been moved by it. Drawn to it. Innately compelled to create it. Now, he knew anything was possible. Love was possible. Passion was motivating. Beauty truly existed.

Ethan picked up his paintbrush and began expressing what was seeking to burst out. With each brush stroke, it was as though he was not just painting, but *expressing*. For the first time since he was young, the paintbrush felt connected to his soul. The bright red, pink, and green coloring depicted the palette of emotions which he felt. The swirling movements of his brushstrokes mirrored how easily he had been swept into the beauty of the moment he so randomly encountered just a couple hours ago.

As he painted, the minutes and hours of the evening ticked by with timeless ease – just as time did not exist when he first met Rose. But despite the longevity of time it took to paint his creation, Ethan did not actually feel time. He did not overanalyze anything about this painting. He just created it – as though every moment from his past and every emotion he'd ever felt culminated in this one creation. Indeed, he didn't want for this moment of unity between himself and art to end, no matter how long it carried him into the night.

But eventually it did end. And in the moment that it ended, Ethan was hit by both sadness of its finality and by exuberance for what he had created.

Over the years, Ethan had mastered the romantic style of painting. That style required precision and a photo-like reality. He was initially drawn to romanticism due to its focus on shadowing, which was necessary to depict the realism of the style. After all the years painting romantic works, Ethan still loved that style because it was the perfect mixture of technique and emotion.

But what he was staring at now conveyed more emotion and awe compared to anything he had ever painted before. And it was all because of Rose. Not because of how excited he was to meet her. And not because she had impressed him beyond words with how poignantly she interpreted his painting. It was because of how intrinsically beautiful she was, and he had recognized her beauty even before she said a word to him.

He'd seen it first out of the corner of his eye from down the hallway of his gallery. He noticed her bright red hair as she stood several feet away. He didn't even know anything about her, like her age, but her beauty had instantly radiated like a flower among thorns.

Ethan's work on his new creation was now finished. It hung in front of him like an emblem to his soul.

For the first time since he'd recreated The Starry Night so long ago, he was no longer intimidated by the impressionist style. Now, he understood it. And he didn't just understand it, he created it. Unlike all of his other paintings, his new one was unique – a one-of-a-kind. It was impressionist.

Now he more fully understood the difference between romanticism and impressionism. Romanticism was first about style, and secondly about emotion. Impressionism cast style to the side and flowed out from the depth of an artist's soul. There was no textbook on creating an impressionist painting, which is why he found it so hard to paint one growing up. All those years back, he had been trying to just learn how to paint, and did so by mimicking other artist's impressionist works. That was a recipe for failure, as it didn't allow him an opportunity to mimic what those artists had been feeling. A painting is more than brushstrokes. And Ethan just learned this, really, for the first time.

Before Ethan hung his first true work of art. He felt it to

be so great, indeed, that he consciously decided at that moment to never again paint another impressionist work. Nothing would ever live up to what he just created. It was that expressive. That perfect. That beautiful.

In front of Ethan hung a painting of a rose.

Chapter 6

"You're early!" Rose yelled to Ethan down the sidewalk as they both approached Sweet Shop Café at the same time. She ran up and put her arms around his neck. Ethan was relieved. Their instant chemistry was just as strong as the night before. Nothing felt different since they'd met just yesterday.

"Are you kidding?" He said while they hugged. "I couldn't wait."

When she pulled away, he reached out and held her hand while they walked into the shop. But Rose had looked him in the eyes long enough to tell that something was on his mind.

"So what's up, Mr. Artist?"

"What?" Ethan genuinely didn't know what she was talking about.

"Oh, c'mon. I see it in your eye. Something's on your mind – spill it."

Rose was right. For as much as Ethan could not wait to see Rose again, a new mistress had captivated him in the interim. He wanted to gush about how he stayed up all night painting his greatest work of art that he would ever create. But he chose not to. He didn't know why, but it just didn't feel right to talk about that. So, instead, he chose to focus on the other greatest work of art in his life – Rose.

"Honestly, I just couldn't wait to see you again." Ethan's direct sincerity was a stark contrast with Rose's playfully flirtatious tone. Though she appreciated that sincerity, she still recognized that she'd just met the man.

"… You see, Mr. Sincerity, you're still a mystery to me."

"Why do you do that – call me by different nicknames?"

Ethan's question would probably cause a lot of people to pause before answering, but Rose's excitement only picked up at being challenged, just as it had the night before. "You're direct, aren't you?" She didn't let Ethan respond before her tone became more serious. "Honestly, I think most people have many sides to them. A name is wonderful, but I guess I just like to point out their different traits sometimes through nicknames. It's nothing personal."

Ethan smiled. Afraid that he'd accidentally offended her with his question, he tried his best to flirt to try and ease things. "I love that, Ms. Observant – don't ever change that about you."

"Ms. Observant, huh?" Rose smirked back. "Sounds like you've spent way too much time in your art gallery."

Ethan wasn't going to contest that. He had – for, like, the last ten years.

As they walked into the café still holding hands, Rose continued. "So, now it's my turn to play a game with you."

"Game, huh?" Ethan said, excited that Rose was now challenging him in response to their game from last night. "Alright – I'm down. What do you got?" Already, Rose's lively initiative was making him loosen up from his rigid artsy self. But what he didn't know yet was that Rose's game would challenge him to do it even more.

"For the rest of the night, you can't talk about painting or your art gallery anymore. I want to know who you are besides that."

Ethan squinted at Rose, but not in disdain. He reveled in her excitable energy and desire to actually get to know him. Besides, she'd already proved that she understood his artist side. If all it took to really draw her in so that she was in his life was to show that there was more to him than art, then he welcomed the challenge. The only thing was, he honestly didn't really have a clue how to do that.

"Okay, but just like last night's game – this one is also two-sided." He suggested.

"Really?" Rose smiled while leaning into him. Just holding his hand no longer satisfied her craving to feel him – she had to get physically closer to him.

They both ordered ice cream from the cafe, enjoying the moment of being close. But the split second of letting go of each other's hands while Ethan paid the cashier was like fate being ripped apart. If even just for the brief moment, they'd both felt it. Holding their ice cream in opposite hands, they both mutually went back to holding hands again like two magnets in the same vicinity instantly attracting.

Walking outside on the warm autumn evening, Rose again resumed their game. "So, you were saying?"

"Saying…."

"Well, what is my side of the game? How can I win it?"

"Help me." He said bluntly.

Ethan had done such a good job loosening up so far during their date that his return to being direct startled Rose. "… help you with what?"

"Help me not think about painting – even if just for one night. Somehow, I don't know how."

"It sounds like we either both win, or we both lose this game, then – right?" Rose's voice cracked in vulnerability in whether Ethan would want them to join forces, even for something as mundane as their made up game.

"I'd be on your team any day – and every day."

Rose returned to her excitable self, feeling confidence from Ethan.

"Well …" She stuttered aloud, looking around for anything that she could use to try and help win the game with him by keeping Ethan's mind off of painting. Her eyes shifted to her surroundings, looking for anything as they walked down the sidewalk in the beautiful autumn night air. "There!" She practically yelled out.

She let go of Ethan's hand and pointed to a marquee on an old musical venue across the street.

"There?" Ethan asked rhetorically, not really sure what was going on.

"Yes, let's go!"

"I mean, sure – if you think that'll help us win the game…" Through his cluelessness of what to expect, Ethan was just following her lead.

"I've never actually heard the music," Rose said in

excitement, willing to try something new. "But I hear it's the next huge act."

They walked across the street, again hand in hand. On the other side of the street, on top of the concert venue, hung a marquee that read "Guy + Guitar."

Chapter 7

As soon as they entered the venue, noise filled Ethan's ears. He didn't like it, but still tolerated it to try and win Rose over. That noise slowly turned into music once they entered the actual room with the band playing.

"Is this Guy Plus Guitar?" Ethan practically yelled into Rose's ear. The floor of the concert hall was packed to the brim with people, so Ethan moved to holding his date from behind. He did not mind this at all, as now he had an excellent reason to draw her in tightly while wrapping his arms around the front of her.

"I doubt it," Rose yelled back. "This is probably the opening act."

"Opening act?" Ethan's lack of experience in music just became apparent.

Upon being asked that, Rose spun around to face him. They stood there, close to each other, and swaying calmly with the sea of people surrounding them who were moving with the music. Even though Rose was now facing him, Ethan didn't change his embrace around her.

"Opening act? Ethan, have you ever been to a concert before?"

The flirty but inquisitive look in Rose's eye had the effect of sucking the truth out of Ethan. "Nope – this is my first time. Any tips?"

"Just try to enjoy it. Feel the music and let it take you somewhere you've never been before."

"Kinda like …" Ethan was about to say 'painting,' but caught himself just before he made them lose their game. With the sentence hanging in the air, he did the only other thing that came into his mind – because it was now all he wanted to think about. He leaned in and kissed her. As he felt Rose's lips on his, Ethan took her advice. He felt the music at the same time that he felt Rose's touch. And the feeling he got from it transcended his expectations. He did not want the moment to end.

But then Rose pulled away, smiling at him. "You're good at that, ya know." She said.

"What, kissing?"

She shrugged. "I mean, at making it feel like more than a kiss."

Rose's compliment made Ethan realize that he didn't

really know anything about Rose. All this time, his instant, strong magnetism to her was so unexpected that it pretty much didn't even leave him questioning who she was. Their innate, mutual attraction left him willing to accept her regardless of any differences. But as accepting of him and willing to be outgoing that she was, this now made Ethan realize that he didn't know anything about her. Afraid that his absentmindedness could be perceived as narcissism or indifference, he knew that this was the time to try to overcompensate.

"Who are you?" He asked plainly while still holding her in his arms.

The question caught Rose off guard, which was normally a hard thing to do. Her natural energy and excitement for life always seemed to have her ready for anything. Ethan noticed that his question made her skip a beat, and he interpreted it as Rose not having received reciprocal interest in past relationships. If his instinct was true, he was determined to fix this. Not only was she the most beautiful person he knew he would ever meet, but she was the best at balancing him out from his natural tendency to be overly serious. He wanted to give her back emotionally what she had already given him in just the twenty-four hours since they'd met.

"Me? Didn't I tell you? I was just released from prison." Her natural energy shone from the sparkle in her eye. "Yep – I'm a serial killer out on probation."

Ethan leaned in and kissed her briefly again. He interpreted her natural humor as a defense mechanism, which he was guessing was due to her prior relationships not actually being interested in her as a person. Really, she was so beautiful that Ethan was sure that her intrinsic beauty was not what drew most men in to her. But he'd seen it last night as she stared and interpreted his painting. He'd seen her depth and humanism just waiting to burst out. Her quick-witted humorous reactions were not just who she was, but who she thought others wanted her to be. He wasn't going to just accept it like other guys may have superficially done. Just as she balanced him out through her lighthearted energy, he wondered if what she needed was for someone to show genuine interest in who she was.

"C'mon Rose. I meant it. Who are you? Where'd you come from? What are your dreams?"

For as close as the two already were while Ethan held her in the concert crowd, his sincerity made Rose draw physically even closer to him. She felt his genuine interest in her, and it was a new thing for her to feel in a romantic relationship. As she drew closer, this time she was the one to lean in for a quick kiss. It was not only her way to say thank you for pushing her defense mechanism to the side, but also because she had to again feel him on her lips.

When she pulled back away, she looked him in the eye while answering his question. "I was just a normal girl, hoping to one day fall in love with a normal guy. But then I stumbled on the most amazingly talented man, and now I feel like the most amazingly lucky woman."

The two lovers pulsed with the movement of the crowd and the beat of the music, periodically shifting between staring into each other's eyes and passionately kissing. Rose had instantly felt what Ethan also instantly felt. They were meant to be together, and they both knew it.

They focused on each other so long that they didn't even notice that the band had changed. No longer was the opening act playing. Instead, Guy + Guitar had taken stage. The name was on point, as it was just a guy named John and his acoustic guitar. Eventually a drummer joined him. But somehow, the music still seemed so full and emotional as the whole band before him that Ethan and Rose didn't even notice the change.

Song after song, they stood there in each other's arms,

thinking of no one but each other. She divulged the real answer to Ethan's prior questions about herself. She said that she was pretty much a normal twenty-one-year-old. She'd grown up with a normal family in the suburbs of Atlanta – not in a particularly rich or particularly poor place. She'd been a cheerleader at her high school, which perhaps was about the only thing about her that seemed different from most girls' experiences growing up. It was through cheerleading that she met most of her boyfriends, which was probably how she knew things with Ethan would be starkly – and refreshingly – different. She'd spent a year at college, but had taken the year off because she felt like the world had so much more to offer than the confines of a classroom. She wasn't looking to fall in love, though she'd hoped one day to be lucky enough to find a nice, normal guy.

Before last night, she'd never given a single thought to painting, let alone art in general. She only stopped into the art gallery while walking downtown because she saw it was a free event. As she now stood being held by Ethan, she was so happy that his painting had stolen her attention. In the moment that it caught her eye, she was surprised to have been moved by it. Never before had that happened from a painting, picture, or anything else. As she had stared at it before Ethan walked up, she wondered if the feelings which were awoken from the painting were what she'd been looking for. And now, being held in Ethan's arms wasn't just confirmation, but completeness. Her whole life, this was what she was looking for. She didn't even know it – and didn't even realize that she was looking for it – but her symbiotic closeness to Ethan was all that she needed in life. And from the moment that she first looked into Ethan's eyes last night, to now being held in his arms and feeling so close to him, she knew that Ethan felt the same way.

But their moment was suddenly interrupted by what was happening on the stage. The singer-songwriter, John, was being accompanied on stage by the final act of the night, named Chris Avary. The audience cheered even more enthusiastically then they had been as they watched their two favorite acts join together on stage. But as John started singing his final song of the night, a woman walked out behind John to surprise him.

Rose spun around again to see what was happening, as it was obviously surprising to the man on stage singing. Ethan held Rose as they watched the woman pour her heart out to John.

"John - I've lived my life without you for far too long," the woman on stage said while beginning to choke up with emotion. "When I saw your face, I knew my life had changed. It was no longer my life, it was *our life*. Wherever you are, I want you. I need you. John, marry me – will you? Will you marry me, John?"

As with many other people in the crowd, Rose couldn't contain tears of joy while watching such a beautiful and surprising event unfold up on stage. But as everyone around them burst into applause and hollering to congratulate the couple, Ethan tightened his embrace around Rose. She stood in front of him as they both watched the strikingly romantic scene in front of them. Not a word was said between them, but they felt it.

Ethan's whole life, he'd been drawing romantic paintings. And now he wondered if he even knew back then what romanticism actually felt like. For all of the success he'd had commissioning and selling his work, none of his prior romantic paintings seemed to have any real emotional meaning to him now. But now did. This very moment meant more to him – evoked more in him – than any of those works. Of course, though, there was one painting which he felt symbolized this union with Rose more than anything else he painted, but he was working hard to try and not dwell on that. He wanted to prove to Rose that there was more to him than painting.

As Guy + Guitar left the stage for the closing act, Ethan leaned forward and whispered into Rose's ear. "Hey, wanna get outta here?"

Rose nodded and the two moved through the dense crowd to make their way out, holding hands as if their lives depended on it.

"You okay, what's up?" Rose asked as they got outside and began walking down the sidewalk of downtown Atlanta.

"Nothing's up, I just wanted to go for a walk with you." Ethan pulled her in closer as they walked, moving his arm around her waist.

It was the perfect autumn night as they strolled through the streets. Night lights in tall buildings surrounded them, embracing them in the warm fall air. The city was alive, and so were they. Rose and Ethan talked about anything and everything that came to their minds – except painting. Ethan finally got more detail from Rose about where she was from and how she'd grown up. Rose kept making Ethan laugh with sporadic witty remarks that made Ethan think her creativity was just as strong as his – just expressed more strongly through words.

The hue of the streetlamps led their path down the city streets as they made random turns to tour a town they both already knew so well. But tonight, it was different. It felt new. The endlessness of the streetlamps symbolized their newfound endless dreams as they talked all night long.

Eventually they made their way back to the cafe where they'd both parked.

"Guess what?" Rose asked in excitement as they stopped by her car. Ethan again held her in his arms. They leaned so that her back was pressed against her car door.

"Wait, let me guess…" Ethan toyed, "Your serial killer instincts are kicking in."

"You noticed, huh?" She joked. "And unfortunately, my serial killer instincts are stronger than my instincts for love."

She had said it. Love. They both knew it from the moment that they met each other, but now it felt even more real.

Rose's tone turned more serious, as she continued: "No really, guess what – I have good news and I have bad news. Which do you want first?"

"Good news."

A sparkle in Rose's eye appeared. "We won! You went all night without talking about painting! We were in it as a team, so that means we won!"

This was great news, and Ethan was thrilled that she remembered their game. He had worked so hard all night to not let his mind drift to its natural interest. Unfortunately, this also meant that the night for them had come to an end. And this is what Ethan guessed the bad news was.

He leaned in an gave her a quick kiss. "It was all because of you," he said. "It's very easy to be distracted when I'm around you … distracted – in a good way." He knew his attempt to flirt was bordering on cheesy, but he really couldn't help it. Luckily for him, Rose's passion right now was accepting. "And let me guess," Ethan continued, "the bad news is that means the night has come to an end."

Rose smirked. "Ethan – it's more like morning at this point."

Ethan nodded in agreement. It had already been late when they left the concert, and their romantic stroll through the city lasted hours afterwards. "So, what's the bad news then?"

"Well, we never decided what the winner would get."

The Sight of Love

Rose was lost in the depth of Ethan's eyes and the closeness of his embrace as he asked her: "Well, what do you want as your reward, Rose?"

Rose looked him straight in the eyes. Her smirk left, turning into a seriousness she never had been able – or willing - to express with any other boy before Ethan. Initially, she was somewhat hesitant to be bold and say it. But once the words came out, they just felt right. "To never live without you again."

Her heart beat a thousand beats per minute, wondering how Ethan would respond. But his words – and the kiss that followed them – left Rose without a single regret.

"Funny, I was going to say the same thing as my reward."

Chapter 8

A year later, Ethan was busy in his study, focused on painting a new romantic-style painting. Since having painted his impressionist painting that he entitled The Rose, he never attempted to paint in that style again. It was as though he felt that he used the impressionist style to its full extent to help him express the most meaningful moment of his life – meeting Rose. And since then, he knew nothing in his life would ever touch that moment, so there was no need to ever try to return to that style.

He didn't hang The Rose in his art gallery. Nor did he hang it in his studio. Instead, he kept it secretly, but carefully, stashed hidden away from others. It was as though it was his personal masterpiece that he would take out in moments of longing – longing to return to the most precious moment in his life. As Ethan stood staring at his new romantic-style work-in-progress, his thoughts drifted off to The Rose. Now was one of those moments of longing.

He cleaned his brushes and walked back to one of his

storage rooms. He moved a shelf from in front of the wall, revealing the hidden spot where he carefully hid his most favorite creation. The light in the storage room was dim, but it didn't matter. He knew every brush stroke. He raised his hand to touch it. He delicately, but intricately, ran his fingers over the brush strokes. One thing about the impressionist style which he relished was that he used a much thicker paint. This meant his brush strokes were thicker and easier to feel, especially compared to the thin paint used in his other romantic works. When feeling The Rose, he would often close his eyes and just feel the painting, transporting him back to the evening – not the memory of painting it, but the memory of meeting Rose. His memories of the feelings he had while painting The Rose were a gateway to the feelings and memories he had from meeting Rose herself. It made those memories tangible. It made them real – even a year later.

He opened his eyes, and looked at the painting. Then the idea hit him. He was being selfish. As much as those memories were his, art should not be kept in the shadows. Eugene would not support what he was doing by hiding his greatest creation for appreciation by just himself. Eugene felt that art should be accessible to anyone who sought to be moved by it. Only because of Eugene's teachings did Ethan realize that he needed to change what he was doing.

His decision was made. He knew of one of his young former students – Bridgette O'Keefe – that was opening her own studio across town. He was going to ask Bridgette to hang it in her gallery. He knew she would, as she was taking a financial and reputational risk by opening a gallery while she was so young. So, she would probably relish the opportunity to hang anything from him in it.

However, Ethan's decision was to not have it be under his name. No – he didn't want it to seem to the artist community like Bridgette was leeching off his goodwill. That wouldn't help her one bit. Nor did he want it to seem as though his contribution would overshadow her own personal paintings. But he still knew that the sight alone of it would help her gallery by drawing in repeat viewers. For those reasons, Ethan decided it would be hung under a pseudonym – Arnold Olsen – a random name that seemed generic and unassuming. The one condition, of course, would be that he could see it whenever he wanted. Knowing Bridgette, this would be no problem.

"Hey! There you are!" Rose's voice echoed from down the hall outside of the storage room. "You can't hide, you know."

"Hide? Why would I wanna hide from you?"

"Not from me, silly. Tonight's the night you meet my family, remember?"

Of course Ethan remembered. It's all he could think about for the last week since they set up the dinner plans. It's the only reason he wore a suit and tie all day, just waiting anxiously to meet Rose's parents. He'd kept it a secret from her, but if everything went right tonight, he was planning to propose in the next couple of weeks. He'd picked out the ring and everything. He just wanted her parents to meet him first. Ethan was sure that the fact he was the owner of a famous downtown art gallery would win their approval despite his younger age.

Rose walked over and straightened up his tie to give him confidence. "I can see it in your eyes, Ethan, don't worry."

"I know..." He said, trailing off. "... it's just that..." He didn't want to spill the fact that he was going to propose soon if it all went well, so he came up with something else to say. "...well, what if – I don't know ... what if they just don't approve?"

"Approve?" She said while smirking. She leaned in and pecked his lips. "Well, I approve. And whose opinion matters more? Some old folks you haven't met yet, or mine?"

She was messing with him to give him confidence. And it was working. This is a part of what Ethan loved about Rose so much – her ability to help balance out his seriousness through her witty humor. But it did occur to him that she didn't say her parents would most likely approve of him.

He was about to chime in, but Rose continued to calm his fears. "And remember – just like I told you. They're traditional, especially my father. That's part of why we waited a year for you to meet them, okay? He should like the fact that we've known each other for so long."

The sparkle returned in her eye, telling Ethan that it was always just Rose who he needed to win over. This gave Ethan confidence. This was going to be a good night.

But then the rain came – literally. They stepped outside, being welcomed by the downpour of a heavy storm. Rain was not unusual to Atlanta, but even this storm seemed uncharacteristically strong. Even the weight of the heavy rains, or their water-soaked clothes - did not bring Ethan's hopes down as they drove to her parents' house. He was sitting in the car with the most beautiful, intelligent, and funny woman in the world. Nothing was going to stop him from marrying her.

The rain didn't cease as they pulled up to her parents' house. They ran to the cover of the front porch. No matter how much they tried to shake off the rain from their clothes, they were drenched. But even though they could have been complaining, it didn't matter. Rose looked over to Ethan, looking him in the eyes as his equal. "Ethan, you'll do fine." She kissed his wet cheek, and he turned to kiss her lips, just before the front door opened.

"Come on in from the storm, you two!" Her mother welcomed them at the front door.

Rose hugged her mother as they stepped inside. Ethan gave her a quick hug as well, trying to set a tone of familiarity from the start. "It's great to meet you Mrs. Abernathy."

"No, no – no need to be so formal here." Rose's father said from the hallway as he walked toward them. But even though his words were welcoming, his tone was defensive. And the fact that he didn't go to even shake Ethan's hand let him know that Rose's father would not be so easy to win over. "Martha and Earl are fine. Come on in," he said in a kind of gruff voice.

Ethan knew he would have to be careful with how he approached things this evening, since it seemed like he wouldn't automatically be given the benefit of the doubt from her dad.

And stepping into Rose's house left Ethan feeling like even more of a fish out of water. Just being in a house again where a family had been raised reminded him of the home he grew up in, even though those memories were now in the distant past. As if that wasn't enough to make him feel uneasy, the feeling of the house itself also left him feeling on his toes. Everything about her house was normal – just like her normal middle-class upbringing which Rose explained to him over the last year. However, Ethan was not used to that. He had been raised in a large, probably overly ornate, upper-class house that his neurosurgeon father had provided for them.

Even though there was nothing specific about Rose's home which wasn't welcoming, it was just the fact that this was a much different setting for a home than he was used to. Ethan immediately assumed that Rose's father must have been a blue-collared type worker. There was nothing wrong at all with that, it was just that Ethan didn't have any experience with it to know how to behave or handle things in that setting.

Eating dinner with her family reinforced to Ethan that her parents, indeed, were traditional. Especially her father, whose questions felt more and more like an interview the deeper they went into conversation. Whereas Ethan initially didn't plan on asking Rose's father for his permission to marry her, that formality now felt like a necessity after meeting them.

"And remind me, Ethan, where is it that you work at, again?" Her father questioned.

There wasn't really a feeling of awkwardness that hung over the dinner table, but more a recognition that Ethan's worthiness to date his daughter was being tested. Rose's mother recognized this instantly and sought to allow the two men to talk alone.

"Oh, hey – Rose, have I showed you the kitchen backsplash we installed since you moved out?" Her mother asked, obviously trying to take Rose into the other room.

Rose winked over to Ethan, signaling she knew what was happening and that she wished him good luck.

The two women got up, leaving Ethan and Earl alone. Ethan should have been intimidated, but he surprisingly wasn't. Though he was anxious, he wasn't nervous. In his mind, he imagined a blank canvas in front of him, and he could turn it into anything. All it took was perseverance and patience. Only the canvas in front of him now was what Rose's father thought of him. Ethan could turn this canvas into anything – steer the conversation in any direction to direct Earl's impression of him. Again, all it took was perseverance and patience on his part – just like if he was painting a new piece.

With the girls having left, Earl again asked the question, but this time with a hint of skepticism in his tone. And from what he said, it was obvious that he'd already known the answer. "So I hear that you work at an art gallery, is that right?"

Ethan couldn't tell if Earl was impressed with this or instead somehow taunting him. But he figured that if he showed passion for what he did, then maybe Earl would see his ability to be passionate in life towards Rose. "Oh, yes definitely! That's all I've ever wanted to do."

"And how long have you been working there?"

Ethan didn't really know how to answer because he never really thought of it in terms of the word "work," so he answered truthfully. "Well, I've been going there weekly since I was about nine. And I formally started working there, I guess, when I was a teenager."

"Do you plan to keep working there long-term?" Again, the father's questions were obviously steered more towards an interview than a conversation. And it was becoming clear that Ethan's answers were futile, as Earl sounded as though he'd already made judgment about Ethan.

But Ethan persisted. "Absolutely. Painting … art is a huge part of my life."

Earl paused for just a brief moment, but it was long enough for Ethan to see that Earl was inspecting him. Ethan didn't know if his effort at directing Earl's attention to his desire to follow his passion was coming across as he'd hoped. So he made sure to ask questions about Earl in return.

"And what is it that you do, Earl?"

"Oh, Rose never told you?"

"No … I don't think so. Why, is it a secret – will you have to kill me if you tell me?" Ethan tried to make a joke to lighten the situation, but it fell flat. His feeling of being a fish out of water was manifesting more and more the further he got into conversation with Earl.

Earl didn't even crack a smile, which worried Ethan even more. And the next question from Rose's father certainly added to Ethan's worry, with how direct he was being by dismissing Ethan's question.

"Ethan, why are you really here? You're the first boy that Rose has ever brought home to meet us." But Earl didn't sound like he was really wanting to hear what Ethan had to say.

Instead, it was almost as if he was taunting Ethan – like he knew why Ethan was meeting him, and he was just waiting for Ethan to admit it before he shot him down. Like a bully.

Perseverance and patience, Ethan reminded himself. This was just a blank canvas, and Ethan could turn her father's impression of him into whatever way he directed it. He could get through her father's tough and undeviating line of questioning which left him feeling judged.

"Honestly, Rose doesn't know it, but I'm here to ask your permission to marry your daughter." Ethan chose to meet the directness of Earl's questioning with directness in return. He hoped that such confident directness would be perceived by Earl as sincerity.

Earl didn't hesitate to respond. "Ethan, no." The simple words hung in the air – as if the bully was trying to let them sink into his victim before continuing to beat him down. "I don't think you're right for my daughter."

That actually caught Ethan off guard. But even more than that, it hurt him. Again, just as he had to be patient in painting most of his creations, he had to decide to exercise that patience here. How to react was a choice, and he was choosing to be patient.

In a measured, even tone, Ethan inquired: "Why do you say that?"

"You work in an art gallery. You're only twenty years old, I ..."

"I'm turning twenty one very soon." Ethan cracked by arguing a minor point. But this signaled his inability to hold in his frustration, making him sound like a teenager regardless of how old he was. But even worse was that he showed a sign of weakness toward a bully, which only fed him the response he'd wanted.

"You can't be who she loves. You just can't – I taught her better. You only work at some art thing, and *she's* my *only* child. She and her mother are all that I have. I've worked hard my whole life to provide for them, and now you come to me asking to marry her? No."

Ethan was crushed. He'd hoped that Earl was just being protective of Rose, who was not just his only daughter but only child. He really knew that Earl was being a bully toward him for some inexplicable reason, but Ethan tried to move past that. In his ignorance, he hoped that he could still win Earl over. He tried to use Earl's over-protectiveness of his daughter to his advantage.

"It's undeniable that you love Rose." Ethan started, again choosing to exercise perseverance and patience.

Luckily, this got a grunting reaction from the father.

So Ethan continued: "And your unwavering love for her has motivated you to want nothing more than to provide for her in life." Earl's eyes squinted, listening intently to what the young man was saying, though his crossed arms signaled that his decision was already made. Still, Ethan gave it a shot. "From the moment I met Rose a year ago, I knew my life would change. I love her too, and that love motivates me just as it has motivated you."

"Ethan, you're what, a starving artist? You can't provide for a family that way until you grow up."

The mounting personal attacks threw Ethan over the edge. "I'm not a starving artist." He denied the allegation bluntly.

"Where do you live when you're not at the studio?" Earl's interrogating question was asked, but the tone sounded as though Earl already knew the answer as before.

"I mean … I live at the studio as well," Ethan defiantly confessed. "… but did you know that I don't just work there – I also own it?"

The question was asked, but by then it was too futile. All Rose's father heard was that his daughter's boyfriend was too poor to live any place besides at his work. The battle was already lost, and Ethan's attempt at directing Earl's impression of him had failed. Ethan knew this already just from Earl's look at him.

"Ethan, the answer is no."

A moment of silence rung in the air. Ethan didn't know how to react, as he knew Earl's impression of him to be wrong. Worst yet, though was his unexpected feeling that Earl somehow enjoyed pushing Ethan to the ground. It felt like a high school fight where the jock shoved the artsy kid on the ground, thinking he was somehow superior.

Feelings of confusion and hurt cut Ethan to the core. All he wanted in life was to provide for Rose. All he wanted in life *was* Rose. He'd do anything that was needed for her. His love knew no end – from the moment he met her, all he knew *was* her. Her beauty, intelligence, confidence, and humor were transcendent.

But still, Earl sat across from him – waiting. Something needed to be said. Ethan wanted to erupt in anger, allowing his instinctive feelings to guide his response. Ethan took a breath in. Patience and perseverance.

Despite how unbearably difficult it was, Ethan tried to be calm and not react defensively. "Earl, I'm sorry, but you're wrong."

Ethan wanted to reveal that Eugene's death resulted in a large inheritance passing to him. He wanted to reveal that the only reason he slept at the studio was because he chose to. He wanted to reveal that he was raised in a much nicer suburb of Atlanta than where Earl lived, and that his inheritance from Eugene would make it so that he never would need to raise a family in the same proletariat middle-class style neighborhood that Earl worked so hard to live in.

But he didn't. That would be the easy route. And even worse, he knew it would just provoke Earl. Even though any rational father should jump at someone having the financial means at such a young age to provide for the rest of his life, that type of rational person just was not Earl. Whether out of defensiveness or his natural attitude in life, Earl just wasn't the type to do any listening tonight.

Moreover, Ethan had never revealed his financial wellbeing to Rose, and he didn't want her to find out about it until they were married. This told Ethan that Rose truly loved him for who he was. If she mistakenly thought that he was a starving artist, then that image didn't hold her back from loving him – as it had obviously held her father back from trusting him. So, if Earl was to gain any respect for his daughter's boyfriend, Ethan wanted it to be based on more than his financial status. It was because of this that Ethan left his response to Earl at the simple statement. "Earl, I'm sorry, but you're wrong."

Whether out of coincidence or intention, Rose appeared to end the awkward confrontation.

"Hey, you two." She said while trying to read the situation. And she read it. She saw hurt in Ethan's eyes, signaling to her that the evening should come to an end. "I'd hate to interrupt, but we should get going, Ethan."

Ethan turned and smiled at Rose, welcoming the thought of his meeting with her father coming to an end. The despair from not getting Earl's blessing to marry his daughter still held firm in Ethan's mind.

At the front door, Rose's mom gave him a hug. "So good to meet you, Ethan." She obviously was unaware of the confrontation between him and her husband.

"Great to meet you too, Martha. Thanks for having me

over. You have a beautiful home."

Ethan then turned to Earl. His ability to persevere through the father's disapproval of him was coming to an end. But, still, Ethan worked hard to take the high road. "Good to meet you as well, Earl. Thanks for having me over."

Ethan's effort to gloss over their prior awkward conversation was equally met by Earl's response – which was obviously nothing more than wanting to not show his daughter how he'd just treated her boyfriend. "Good to meet you too, Ethan."

As they turned to return to their car, the rainstorm from earlier had still not let up. What began as an evening where Ethan's hopes had overcome the rain had now become an evening where the rain symbolized his despair.

The drive back into the city was silent, further signaling to Rose that her suspicion was correct that Ethan's conversation with her father did not go well. Ethan's silence, though, was not due to anything besides the fact that he kept replaying the conversation over and over in his mind. He wondered what it was that he did wrong – how he misplayed the situation. After thinking it over for most of the car ride back, the one conclusion he arrived at was that he was never going to get

Earl's blessing. He wasn't sure if it was due to his profession or age – or, perhaps, both. But there was nothing short of divulging the details of his modest wealth which would have won Rose's father over. Ethan didn't blame Earl. Rose was his only daughter, and he'd worked his whole life to provide for her, only to have a twenty-year-old appear blinded by love asking for his only child's hand in marriage. Ethan wasn't going to win.

But still, in replaying the conversation over, there was one detail that Ethan realized he never got. Ethan pulled up to Rose's apartment and parked, finally breaking the silence. The quiet ride back had slowly stirred worry into Rose's mind. She had no clue about what was said between her father and Ethan, and the silence naturally made her wonder if it would spill over to affect her relationship with Ethan. And that was the last thing she wanted.

Ethan's question in breaking the silence both surprised her and somewhat calmed her mind down. Instead of hearing Ethan say something about their relationship, he instead simply asked, "Rose, what does your father do for a living?" That was the one detail from Ethan's conversation which he never got from Earl, and Rose had never told Ethan about her father's job before.

"He works on the assembly line at a steel production plant."

There it was. Ethan understood exactly why Rose's father was so concerned with Ethan's ability to provider for her. Earl was a worker – and obviously a hard worker at that. He'd probably been through many phases of worrying about layoffs, and possibly even lived paycheck to paycheck. It wasn't that Ethan was judging Earl - he never would. Earl's hard work ethic is what helped Rose be the woman that she was today. And Ethan loved her so incredibly much. So, Ethan naturally was grateful, if not indebted, to Earl for the life he worked so hard to provide for his daughter. Earl just had a very different perspective on life than Ethan due to their vastly different professions.

But still, the fact that her father wouldn't even let Ethan explain himself pained Ethan. And on top of that, he was just a bully to him. And that resulted in deep pain that still showed in Ethan's eyes.

Rose saw that pain, and continued: "… I take it things didn't go so well."

Ethan tried to take the high road and downplay the

situation, as much as he wanted to tell Rose everything. But something in his mind figured that if he told her that her father didn't approve of him, then maybe that would throw up a yellow flag in their relationship. The last thing he wanted to do was give Rose a reason to doubt their relationship. So, he lied.

"No, it was fine. Yeah … fine."

"Don't lie to me," Rose immediately chirped back. "You're a bad liar, Ethan. I see it in your eyes."

Just as with Rose's father, Ethan seriously misplayed this conversation as well. He knew he wasn't good with words, but he had more than struck out tonight. He tried to come up with something to say, but it was too late. Rose had given up for the evening.

She opened the car door and got out on the sidewalk in front of her townhouse. She stood in the pouring rain. With the car door ajar, she leaned in to say one last thing before she turned to run through the storm back to her front door. "Don't lie to me Ethan. I'll see you tomorrow – hopefully by then you can tell me the truth."

She shut the door. Ethan watched her retreat toward her front door, sitting alone in his car to collect his thoughts with only the sound of the rain pattering on the hood of his car providing him company.

Then he made the decision. The truth. If she wanted the truth, there was no reason to withhold it from her.

Immediately, Ethan opened his car door and ran through the rain to Rose. He caught her a couple steps before she reached the front door.

"Rose!" He yelled out.

"Rose, I love you!" He yelled it at her from the side of his car as he walked through the rain to reach her.

They had said it several times before, but this time was different.

Rose obviously did not anticipate Ethan putting up a fight to change her mind. She turned around to face him. Her normally wavy, brilliant red curly hair was now weighed down in the rain – pasted to her forehead. "What did you say?"

"I said, I love you."

Ethan reached Rose. He raised his hand and moved her hair from in front of her face.

"I know you do, but why now? Why tell me now?"

"Because you wanted the truth. I love you Rose Abernathy. And I always will."

"No, Ethan. I know you love me. I meant the truth about

what happened with my father. I want *that* truth."

The two lovers stood in the rain. It beat down hard, but it didn't matter to them. All that mattered – all that existed – to them was each other.

"I asked your father for his blessing – for me to marry you. And he said no."

Rose should have been shocked. She should have been shocked that Ethan asked her father the first time he met him. But that didn't even enter her mind. Instead the only thing she could think of was excitement that Ethan felt the same way as she felt about him. It was just them standing in the rain, and she would stand in the rain with Ethan for the rest of their lives if she could. As long as she had him, she didn't care what was happening around them – or if her parents approved.

"Ethan, you don't need his permission. Nothing could ever hold me back from being with you." Ethan stood staring back at her, his blue eyes blending in with the ocean of rain that fell all around them. But still, it was an ocean that Rose wanted to drown in.

This is what Ethan loved about Rose. Though she was naturally an upbeat person, she was unafraid to still express herself passionately towards him. And that gave Ethan all the confidence in the world.

"I love you Rose Abernathy," Ethan yelled in the rain, looking Rose in the eyes. The rain poured hard, and with it now poured Ethan's true feelings to Rose. For the first time since he could remember, he felt like he was actually able to say the words that he felt – he didn't need a paintbrush, Rose was all he needed. "I love you," he repeated again, "and nothing could ever make that change. I love you for who you are today, where you came from, and whoever you are in the future. I want my future to be with you. I want you, Rose – I need you. From the moment I met you – so unexpectedly that night – I knew I needed you."

Ethan knew where his outpour of love was leading, but it was interrupted by Rose. "Ethan, do you believe in love at first sight?" She asked. They had expressed their love for each other before, but tonight felt way beyond those prior moments.

"Do you?" He asked back.

"I didn't until I met you!" She practically had to yell back through the thunderous sound of the rain on the pavement all around them. "But I asked you first, Ethan – do you believe in love at first sight?"

"From the moment I saw you, I knew that I didn't just

believe in love at first sight, but I believed that love could last a lifetime."

Ethan kneeled on the wet pavement, not caring about anything other than the woman standing in front of him. He reached into his pocket and pulled out a ring.

"Rose, I bought this the week I met you. I knew from that first night that I wanted to spend the rest of my life with you. Rose Abernathy, will you marry me?"

A smile an ocean wide came across Rose's face. "Yes!" She couldn't hold back. "Now get up, Ethan!" She took her hand and put it over Ethan's hand which held the ring. She pulled him up to his feet and then jumped up onto his hips. Ethan held her in the rain as she leaned down and kissed him passionately.

"Of course," she said while kissing him over and over. "Yes, Ethan Cooley! Yes, I will marry you!"

Chapter 9

"Alright, so next week, we'll continue with our paintings, okay?" Ethan instructed his class. It was Friday evening and his week of leading his students in painting had come to an end - which meant that he had finally reached the weekend. "Over the weekend I want you to think about the shadowing that needs to happen in your paintings. And come back ready to focus on shadowing much of next week. Remember – what's revealed in the shadows is just as important as what's depicted in the light."

With that, one of his high school student's hand raised.

"Yes, Leila?"

"Well, it's just …" She trailed off.

"Go ahead…"

"Well, how come you only paint in the romantic-era style?"

"Yeah," another student chimed in, asking what was probably on several of the young student's minds. "Is it because you're a newlywed?"

The Sight of Love

The student's questioning made Ethan laugh out loud. He was about to answer, when all of a sudden he heard Rose's voice come from the hallway outside of the classroom in his studio.

"And what's wrong with that?" She asked jokingly. "You guys realized I married the most romantic guy in all of Georgia, right? You're not trying to take that away from me are you?"

The class laughed and Ethan silenced them by dismissing them. "Okay, see you all next week. But remember shadowing over the weekend."

The students all left as Rose walked over and hugged him.

Ethan greeted her: "Well there's my hot date for the evening." He said before kissing her on her lips. "You look stunning!" Rose was wearing a tight black, polka-dotted dress that hugged her at the waist right where a rose-shaped broach was pinned. Rose couldn't hold back a smile, but an idea quickly entered Ethan's mind. "Here – follow me!" Several months of being married to Rose had made her excitable personality rub off on Ethan in this moment.

Rose didn't even have a chance to ask what was going on before Ethan took her hand and led her down his studio hallway. They entered the art gallery and passed the hallways where many of the classics hung, largely undisturbed from the days when Eugene owned the gallery. They walked down to the last hall where Ethan hung several of his paintings. Ethan briskly led the way, with Rose being unsure of what was happening.

But where Ethan stopped gave Rose a clue about his intentions. He placed her right in front of the one painting of his that he never moved, 'Embrace the Light.' It was the same exact painting that he saw Rose standing in front of the evening that he first met her.

"Okay, right about there," Ethan said as he let go of her hand and ran down the hallway. He spun around and looked down at her.

"What are you doing?" Rose giggled as she yelled to her husband down the hall.

"Just … don't move for a moment, okay?"

"Alright," she murmured to herself in humor. She turned back to look at the painting which had started it all between them – leaving Ethan up to whatever it was that he was doing. She figured he was kicking their date off by going down memory lane, but seeing this painting again distracted her mind from Ethan's intentions. She turned, standing in high heels under the dim lights which illuminated the paintings all around her. The feelings which this painting evoked had not only surprised her that night so long ago, but were now resurfacing. She'd never really been into art until this one stood out to her. But, now, as Rose stood surrounded by several of Ethan's paintings, she realized that she was moved by more than just this one.

Ethan stood down the hall, staring at her. Yes, he was going down memory lane, but it was a road he relished. Seeing his tall rose standing there, her red curly hair mirroring a beautiful rose in the wild, was a scene that he'd been so moved by those couple of years ago, that it led to his greatest painting of all that same evening he met her. Even though recreating her beauty through painting it should have helped him move on from the moment, the image of her beauty standing there never left his mind. Rather, it'd only become magnified over time.

Only tonight, she was wearing a stunning black, polka-dot dress, and he was now trying his hand at being romantic not just with a paintbrush – but with his words.

"That's it!" He yelled down to Rose, who practically jumped at his words after having been distracted by the paintings all around her.

"That's, what?" She yelled back.

"I know the answer now!" He said to her as he began walking down the hallway to her. When he reached where she was standing, he reached his arms out and placed them around her waist, enjoying the feeling of her in his arms.

"Know the answer to what?" She asked. She knew he was being coy as a form of flirting with him, and she reveled in every moment of it.

"Well," Ethan explained. "It's just that it took me about a year to propose to you after seeing you in the green dress."

Rose didn't know where this attempt at flattery was going.

"And you look so stunning in this dress tonight that I had to see…"

"See what?"

"Well, if you had been standing there the night I met you, wearing this black dress instead, could I have been able to wait a whole year to propose?" Ethan smiled at her in his arms, and Rose smirked back after seeing where this was going. "And the answer is definitely no. I wouldn't have been able to wait a whole year if you'd been wearing this when I met you."

Rose chuckled.

"In fact, I probably would have proposed to you right

there on the spot. I just wouldn't have been able to hold it in."

Rose was flattered, but also willing to flirtatiously play back at her husband. "Well, maybe that's what my serial killer tendencies intended?" She flirted back, referencing to her joke from the night of their first date. "Maybe I'm still in it for the hunt – just waiting for you to let your guard down. You were getting suspicious of me, so I had to marry you."

Ethan always loved this joking-flirtatious mood of Rose's, just as much as he loved it when she turned passionately serious. Over the last couple years, this joking mood had brought the same thing out in Ethan, providing him balance which he never really knew he needed before meeting her.

"Well, one thing's for sure…" He began. While being held by Ethan, Rose leaned in to hear if Ethan would continue with her playful banter. "… you certainly would have killed me with your looks that night if you were wearing this dress."

What a line, Rose thought. Look at this man who was holding her. What she said to his class was right – she may have just found what turned out to be the most romantic man in all of Georgia. She was his. This man who used to express himself so poignantly on canvas, yet had trouble expressing himself verbally, had now grown to be able to equally express himself in words – ever since the night when Ethan poured his heart out to her in the rain and proposed.

But Rose knew she had to match his quick wit. "Well, I guess it's a good thing I wasn't wearing this dress, then."

"What? Why's that?"

"Because I'm starting to like this whole marriage thing – even if it only started as a way for me to get close to you."

Ethan leaned in and kissed Rose. When he pulled away, she turned to the wall of his paintings next to them.

"You know, for as much as I liked your paintings from before I met you, you've gotten even better since then."

"Oh, stop it," Ethan said, figuring that she was just trying to compliment him.

"No, I mean it, babe." She insisted. "I mean, look at this one."

They walked down the line of paintings stopped right in front of one called "Emblem of Your Soul." Ethan looked at it and remembered the days it took him to paint it. He had painted it about six months after meeting Rose. He didn't know why, but he felt the scene just leak out of his imagination. It wasn't as strong of an impression as when he painted The Rose from the evening that they met, but then again, he didn't think that anything he'd ever paint again would be.

"You like this one, huh? He asked while holding her hand. The feeling of her fingers intertwined with his was as fresh and as exciting of a connection as the night they met.

"I like all of yours, Ethan. I really do. But this one was obviously painted after we met."

"Really? How can you tell?"

"Well ..." she began while staring at it. Ethan stood just behind her side enough for it to look like he was also inspecting his painting. But really, what he was inspecting was his wife. It was that same, honest intrigue that she had the evening they met, when she interpreted his painting without even knowing he was the painter. The fact that she still had that same spark about her when looking at his art this evening told him that her interest and intrigue from it was genuine. This was a rare thing for a person to display, as he knew from seeing thousands of visitors walk the halls of his gallery.

Rose's interpretation continued: "... well, it's just that there's so much more depth to your work since we met. It's like your earlier works were technically proficient, but your recent works have evoked more emotion. They're more inspired. More real. And so they're easier to connect with."

"I agree," Ethan said. "They are evoked by emotion more. I wonder why…" He kissed his wife on the forehead. "I guess one could say that I'm not the only painter of it anymore."

For as much as Rose appreciated the compliment, her critique wasn't over. "Thanks, babe. But, I mean it. I mean look at Emblem of Your Soul. What were you thinking when you created it? What was your motivation? What were you trying to convey?"

Ethan could have easily explained everything to her. But, he was impressed by Rose's innate draw to his work. He wondered if this was how Eugene had felt all those years ago when he met him, so Ethan decided to do the same thing Eugene did to him. Ask what Rose saw in it.

"Well, what do you see? What do you think I was trying to convey?"

Rose immediately answered the question, as if she was just waiting to be asked. "You see how the painting initially appears to be a couple in the middle of a grass field?"

Ethan again stood staring at his wife. "Yes…" Of course he knew what it was. The painting showed a man holding a woman up by the waist in the middle of the golden grass field on a sunny day, with the wind slightly blowing the woman's long dress behind her, flowing with the top of the grasses.

"You see how the wind carries the dress, grass, and clouds with it to the right of the picture?" She no longer was waiting for Ethan's response. "Well, what you can barely see perched on the hillside in the background is a white house with a large front porch."

Now Ethan was intrigued. She'd noticed something about the painting which he intentionally made look insignificant. Rose was onto something, which peaked his interest.

"You called it Emblem of Your Soul. But, why?" She turned and looked at her husband for a second, as if looking at the creator might help channel her ability to interpret the creation. "I think it's because the couple is not the sole point of the painting."

"Rose, are you saying I value something above you?" He taunted, almost intentionally trying to steer her critique off course.

"Are you saying that's us?" She asked in a serious tone. "Because I don't have brown hair." She nudged Ethan, letting him know she understood that all of his paintings couldn't be an exact replica of them, otherwise the hall would look more like a stairwell of family portraits instead of an art gallery.

She continued, again seriously. "No, really, I mean - what I see is that there's more to this painting than just a happy couple engulfed in each other on a beautiful day. You called it Emblem of Your Soul – but an emblem is a thing. A woman isn't a thing – *I'm* not a thing, and I know you've never seen me as just a thing, but a real person. So, then I ask, *what* is the emblem of your soul?"

"And …?"

"And I think the key is the house. It's a large house with a large porch. Next to it is a tree with a tire swing. The feeling I get from the house is that there's a family living there. This couple is not alone – they're parents. And they've found a moment of freedom from the cares of the world, from the stresses of parenting, to enjoy each other unrestrained and on a beautiful afternoon."

She turned and looked at Ethan. "I think what you're trying to say is that freedom is the emblem of your soul. Because all you've ever sought is to express yourself freely." She paused. Her seriousness turned into a smile, like a test just ended and she was waiting to find out if she passed. "I mean – am I right?"

Now Ethan was smiling. It was his turn to have some fun with Rose. He could say anything because only he knew the true meaning of the scene. "I give you an A..." He started. When she smiled like she had won, his trailing sentence finished in a way that surprised Rose. "... A *minus*."

"A minus! No – you're just messing with me. What did I get wrong?"

"You know, Rose, you say that you never had any interest or training in art before the night I met you. But I gotta tell you, if you were in my classes, you'd be at the head of them."

Rose rolled her eyes, when she heard his flattery.

"No, I really mean it!" He insisted. "I painted this in front of my class as a way to show them the use of coloring. The brown in the woman's hair, the yellow of the sunlight, the golden grasses, and the white on the house – these were very difficult to do with enough distinctiveness. They followed along painting their recreation of my example."

"So, that's it? Just the use of colors? I read too much into it then, I guess..."

But Ethan immediately corrected her. "No, Rose. That's why I painted it in front of the class – as a lesson in the contrast of colors and effectiveness of shadowing. But what I didn't tell them was that the real reason I painted it was to express…"

"Express what?" Rose's curiosity burst out.

"Express my use of symbolism through the wind – just as you caught wind of." He smiled at her, waiting for her to pick up on his pun. "Get it? You caught wind of my use of the wind in it?"

It took a second, but Rose chuckled out loud when she finally got it. "So, I'm right then? What the wind is pointing to and what the emblem of your soul was?"

"Well, not quite. You are so close. Like I said A minus."

Ethan's attention again turned from the painting to looking at his wife while he explained the rest of the meaning.

"You see, the house is large enough for a family. But just as much as I tried to hide the house which the wind points toward, I hid other things in this painting as well."

Rose let go of his hand and stepped forward to inspect it even closer.

"Remember the point of this painting wasn't just about how to use the colors, but also how to contrast them through use of shadows. Look in the shadowing of the tall grasses."

He gave Rose a minute to look for his hidden clues.

"It's what lies in the shadows, Rose, that creates the true

beauty of this painting. The shadows give away the key to what's the emblem of my soul."

Rose squinted, and Ethan would have been seriously impressed if she saw what he so skillfully and artfully sought to hide within the tall golden grasses.

"I see them!" Rose exclaimed, much to Ethan's surprise.

"What do you see?"

"I see the faces and clothes of three children running around the man as he holds the woman in the air!"

Rose stood still for just a moment, digesting what she just said out loud. Suddenly, she turned to her husband. "That's it!"

Ethan couldn't hide it any longer. His objective enthusiasm was spilling out at his wife's unique ability to interpret even the most hidden intentions of his creations. "What, Rose? What do you see?"

"It's not freedom that's the emblem of your soul. It's family!"

He leaned over and kissed his wife on the head again. "You're so incredibly close. You get an A for sure, but not quite an A plus yet."

Without waiting for Rose to question what she was missing, Ethan instinctively filled in the gap. "The Emblem of

My Soul was the freedom that can come from a loving family."

Rose had been married to Ethan for several months, but he could still make her blush. Between his earlier compliment of her dress and now knowing that he wanted a family with her only about six months after being married, she was in love with the man before her. And it was an insane, mad love – one which she was glad she decided to keep close to her for a lifetime.

Chapter 10

Rose leaned over and kissed Ethan. The kiss lingered longer than she intended, because just the feeling of Ethan's lips transported her to a scene beyond the romanticism portrayed in his paintings. When they broke off, the excitement in her eye returned.

"So, you still wanna go on that date, Mr. Family Man?" The fact that she called him that surprised her. They'd never spoken about having a family before, and just saying that out loud made her a bit nervous. She'd always imagined that she'd have a family, but she just didn't know how he would react. This could have been because Ethan never wanted to talk about his own family, so she figured that the topic of family in general was off limits for some reason. So, once the words spilled out accidentally, she inspected Ethan's reaction to try and get a sense of how he felt on the subject – the fact that Ethan had already drawn a whole painting about it wasn't enough for her at this moment.

But Ethan didn't even balk at the name, instead talking

about their date. "I mean, babe – I'm not gonna lie…"

"What? Let me guess – you wanna cut the date short and just go home early, now – right?" She rolled her eyes.

"No, no – it's not that." Ethan corrected her. "It's just that I'm not in the mood to go to a movie tonight," he admitted. Worried that he was letting her down, he continued. "I mean, we can if you want. But it's just that I'd rather do something where we can actually talk."

"Kinda like we just did with your art?"

"I mean, yeah – kinda like that." He leaned in and kissed Rose on the lips. "I love talking to you, Honey. Let's find something else to do tonight, okay?"

If her husband wanted to actually talk to her, then that was a request Rose was going to accept. Besides, Rose knew her husband. She knew he was in one mood – the mood to pursue his only other passion besides her in life. He wanted to talk about painting. She'd worked so hard since they met at giving him other interests and things to focus on. And he'd done so good at balancing himself out. So, she figured there was no harm in letting up on him for an evening every once in a while by taking him to other galleries. Besides, she was already kinda in the mood to do that after enjoying their conversation about his painting.

Rose's eyes sparkled with excitement when an idea hit her. She still wanted to get Ethan out of his element a little, and she knew what might work.

"Ethan, you know how I'm always saying that you should branch out to appreciate other styles of art?"

"Oh, but I do …" Ethan reacted somewhat defensively.

"I know, I know. I said that wrong. It's just that you spend so much time in your own gallery, that I thought – well, if you wanna get out and look at art, your former student Bridgette O'Keefe has a newer gallery we could go to."

This was a shock to Ethan. One which he hoped didn't backfire. His wife had no idea that he would frequent Bridgette's gallery on the other side of town to see his most prized painting – The Rose. For a split second, Ethan felt as though he'd been cheating on his wife behind her back and she just found out. Ethan had been travelling to see it several times a month without telling his wife. It wasn't really cheating, but his secrecy still led to Ethan feeling off guard when Rose suggested it.

Then Ethan had an idea. He was curious. If Rose didn't know that he painted it, how would she react when she saw it?

The thought burned in his mind, and he was glad that he'd chosen to donate it to Bridgette under a pseudonym. Ethan couldn't stop wondering about what the motivation behind his only impressionist painting would think of his creation that blossomed from having met her.

"I mean, I guess it would be a good thing to support her," Ethan said. Giving the air of reluctance was part of his act to pretend that he wasn't the painter behind The Rose.

But Rose wasn't really excited at his reaction, instead looking somewhat disappointed by Ethan's mediocre response to her idea. Ethan caught wind of this, though, and immediately leaned in to kiss her again.

This time, he sounded much more excited and supportive. "Let's do it! I actually like the idea."

In the car, Rose's mind drifted to her earlier interpretation of her husband's Emblem of Your Soul painting.

"Ethan – did you really mean it?"

"Yeah! I think seeing Bridgette's gallery is a great idea…"

"No, Ethan – I mean what you said about the Emblem of Your Soul? Did you mean that freedom from having a loving family was really the emblem of your soul, or was it just an idea that you wanted to express?"

Ethan glanced over at his wife seated next to him in the car. "I meant it. I still mean it." He smiled briefly at her before looking back at the road. Even though he looked back, he still placed his right hand on hers near the car's middle console, just holding her hand for a moment.

Rose could always sense Ethan's sincerity, and his response was definitely one of those times. She felt warm, and was no longer worried about earlier calling him Mr. Family Man. She was thrilled to have received this reaction from Ethan. But then her mind went to one potential explanation for Ethan's value in family.

As if a knife cut through the air, gutting Ethan unexpectedly, Rose simply said: "I'm actually relieved. I was worried that you'd never want a family because you've never wanted to speak about your own one." She looked out the window, unaware of the impact of her words which she spoke so matter-of-factly. "Sometimes I wonder what they're like and why they cut you off."

Ethan stirred in his seat as he drove. Of everything in life, this was his most dreaded topic. Thinking about his family was the last thing he ever wanted to do – the pain from them never reaching out to him was too deep for him to think about sometimes. So, talking about it with Rose was something he always sought to avoid. And thus far, he had managed pretty well at avoiding the topic.

Naturally, Rose had inquired about meeting his parents after they got engaged. But by that point, Ethan had consciously decided to cut them off completely. He figured that they'd never once come to visit him at his gallery despite his open invitation. They never even called him. So, he decided that they were essentially dead to him. He'd told Rose that his family was completely out of the picture – figuring that doing so would quell any attempts by her to try to reunite them. And it did. Of course, he wanted to try and have some type of relationship with his parents and siblings, and it pained him that none of them ever sought to have a relationship with him once he moved to the gallery.

Instead of going further into the subject, Ethan just chose the path of least emotional resistance by trying to avoid it yet again: "Yeah … too bad."

Their arrival at Bridgette's gallery saved Ethan from needing to say a word more.

They got out of the car, and Rose walked over to her

husband. Before holding his hand, she straightened his collar and pecked him on the lips. "Try to enjoy it even though it's not your gallery or paintings, okay?" The excitement sparkled in Rose's eye, and Ethan mirrored the feeling due to the excitement of wondering how Rose would react to his painting.

As they entered Bridgette's gallery, he broke off from Rose. "Hey, I'm gonna go say hi to Bridgette for a second. I'll come find you, okay?"

Of course Ethan really had another reason for wanting to immediately find his former student. He had to catch Bridgette before she saw them looking at his painting. Bridgette had to be in on this, too, if he was going to discover his wife's true thoughts about his impressionist painting.

"I love the idea!" Bridgette exclaimed once he found her. "I'm glad you let me know – I won't say a word about it. And I'll leave you two alone then." Bingo. The plan was initiated.

And it was a plan which did not take long at all to unfold. Leaving Bridgette, Ethan went to search for his wife, only to quickly find her standing exactly where he'd hoped they would end up by the end of the date.

There she was. Down the hall, standing under the dim

light in front of his painting. Wearing that black polka-dot dress with her red wavy hair standing brilliantly as a symbol of the beauty and independence which she held inside as well. He'd been married to her for several months and known her now for about two years, yet there she still stood – breathtaking in every way imaginable.

Lucky. That was the first word that entered Ethan's mind. He was lucky to have found this delicate rose amid the weeds and chaos of the rest of the world. He was lucky that she had become the unique woman she was despite her otherwise normal upbringing. And he was lucky to have been able to marry her despite her family's initial – and continued – reluctance toward him. He was the luckiest man in the world because, to Ethan, the world only really consisted of Rose and himself.

Ethan was right about what he said back in his gallery when describing her in that black polka-dot dress. If he didn't know who she was before tonight – if this was the evening which he had first seen her – he would not be able to withhold himself from thrusting himself into her world.

And it wasn't the fact that she had chosen to stop in front of his painting which motivated these feelings. It was her beauty. She could be standing in front of a blank white wall, and it wouldn't have mattered. The dim of the gallery light wasn't there to illuminate the painting. *She* was the work of art which it shone down to display. He was fortunate to have known that there was such depth behind her light. Even her shadows were magnificently beautiful.

"What do you see?" He asked casually while approaching her from down the hall, pretending not to know what she was looking at.

Rose stood still not saying a word – just looking at it.

"What is it?" Ethan again prodded. "I haven't seen that look in you since the night I met you."

Rose smiled at Ethan as he approached more closely. She reached out and grabbed hold of his hand, drawing him in. He turned to see what she was looking at, but he knew already. He'd come here often and knew exactly where his painting The Rose was hanging.

"What do *you* see?" She asked Ethan.

"Nope. I asked you first."

The glimmer of transcendence shined bright in her eyes. Her excitement was palpable as she unknowingly described the pinnacle of Ethan's creation which he had painted the same evening he met her.

Rose turned and looked at The Rose, pausing a moment before speaking again. "I feel like I'm staring into a mirror."

Ethan felt deeply complimented by her heartfelt initial reaction. He never painted it hoping that she'd critique it one day. He painted it for himself, as though the very semblance of his being needed to be expressed onto canvas. Now, fate ended up having Rose feel that same expression – without even knowing that he was the creator.

But he didn't want to let on yet that it was him, so he tested her sincerity. "Funny joke, Rose. I get it – it's a picture of a rose so you feel like you're staring into a mirror…"

Ethan barely finished his sentence before Rose immediately interrupted. "No, Ethan. That's not it. I'm not joking. Look at it … it's *depth*. Each pedal stands out as so unique but also so much apart of the entirety of the rose as a whole. It's as though each moment that it took to create each pedal held its own significance but helps to create the larger flower. And the beauty of the flower is … is … well – I can't quite explain it."

Ethan stood staring alongside his wife. He knew what she was saying. He'd felt it the moment he stood back and saw what he painted, and he felt it the first time he saw Rose that evening so long ago.

So Ethan took over the critique. "I'm guessing its beauty struck you immediately."

"Yes!"

"I'm guessing you noticed the waviness and brilliance of each pedal, but yet also simultaneously was struck by the beauty of the entire rose."

"Yes!"

"And it's a lingering but striking beauty that grabs hold of you, penetrating deep into your soul, and you never want it to let go. You could see how you could just stand and dwell on it for long periods of time, and wondering if you would ever be the same now that you've been touched by the indescribable feeling which it has summoned from inside of you."

"Yes!" She again almost yelled, as if the objective truth of those statements could not be denied. Then she turned and looked to Ethan at her side, still holding hands. "... How did you know?"

Ethan was tempted to give it all away. To tell her he painted this the night he met yet her, and that he knew because it reflected what he saw in her that evening and every day since.

But he didn't. Something told him to hold that information back – as if saying it would diminish or taint what she saw in the painting.

"Because I see it too," Ethan said while now looking Rose in the eyes. He was unsure of whether he was talking about her or the painting, but it didn't matter. It was true regardless.

Rose's excitement changed from being emotionally moved by the painting to her excitement about Ethan's appreciation of it. "You did it!" She exclaimed, moving close to him.

"Did … what?"

"See? I knew you could appreciate something besides the romantic-era style."

"Oh c'mon, Rose. You know I can. I have many, many paintings from all other eras hanging in my gallery."

"I know, but have you ever heard of this artist before … Arnold Olsen?"

"No."

"And yet here you are being so incredibly moved by it. So … you did it, Ethan! This isn't one of the classics hanging in your halls. This is a modern, unknown artist whom you've discovered – not based on his reputation, but on the actual creation itself."

"I like that word." Ethan steered away from her compliment back to yearning to hear what his wife thought of the painting.

Rose was momentarily caught off guard, but took a second to dwell on Ethan's comment.

"Creation?" She asked.

"Yeah."

"Why do you like it?"

"I don't know … you said it. I just like it." Ethan's statement from left field left Rose in thought for a second as she dwelled on why she'd called it a creation instead of a painting. So Ethan continued: "What do you think he was feeling the night that this … Arnold Olsen … created The Rose? What do you think he was trying to convey?"

Ethan had intentionally steered Rose back to his painting by asking the same questions he asked her earlier in the night when staring at his Emblem of Your Soul painting. The glimmer in Rose's eye showed that her excitement was still just as earnest as it was earlier in the night with that painting. But unlike earlier in the night, her words now were much more concise.

"I think Arnold Olsen saw a glimpse of something timeless, and he would have gone crazy if he didn't try to recreate it."

Rose then returned from her trance and inquired of Ethan: "Do you ever get that way when you create something?"

"How?"

"Like you'll go crazy if you don't share what you've created. Like there's an initial nervousness at the sheer magnitude of the initial task, hoping that you don't make mistakes, and hoping that in the end it'll all be alright – it'll be worth it."

Something was different in Rose. For as good as she was at reading her husband, the tone in her description stood out to Ethan now. She was nervous about something, but he couldn't read her to know what was going on.

"Rose, are you alright?" He asked.

The nervousness in her voice trembled down into her hand. Ethan felt her shaking. She cracked a half smile when divulging her next words in uncertainty.

"Ethan, I'm pregnant."

The entire night flashed back before Ethan's eyes. All

the talk about family being the emblem of his soul. Rose calling him Mr. Family Man. And Rose questioning him about creating something. It all made sense now, like the final puzzle piece to his wife was now put down. She was pregnant, and hadn't known how to tell him.

But not only was she pregnant, she was clearly nervous about it. Ethan wasn't sure if she was nervous because it was a new thing, or if she was nervous at how he would react. But one thing he knew – he needed to say something quick or she might interpret his silence as non-approval.

In the split second he had to react, all of these emotions were processed quickly. But one emotion stood out from all the others – she was pregnant! His excitement rose to the surface, needing to be expressed just as much as Rose needed to express her appreciation of his painting as an undeniable truth.

Ethan broke into a huge smile. "Really?" He asked excitedly. Rose nodded her head nervously. He couldn't help but grab her head and pull her in to kiss her, signally his approval and excitement. He broke away after a few long seconds. "You're pregnant!"

Rose's nervousness turned into a reassured, now also excited smile, relieved at Ethan's response.

Ethan instinctively put both of his arms around his wife. Grabbing hold of her around her waist, he raised her up and spun her around in pure joy and celebration. "We're pregnant!" He yelled again.

But then a sudden look of regret and caution crossed his face. He put her down. "Oh, sorry," he said while holding his hand out to her stomach. "I hope I didn't hurt him … or her! I shouldn't have done that."

Rose chuckled. "I think that's okay. It's still really early."

The electric excitement still couldn't be withheld by Ethan. He had to tell someone – he wanted to tell the whole world, but instead the art gallery patrons would have to do. He raised his hands to form a cup around his mouth while yelling into the gallery. "Hey everyone – she's pregnant! I'm gonna be a dad!"

Random clapping broke out from the other side of the gallery walls. In only a moment's time, Bridgette came from around the corner toward them. "Congrats you two!" She said with a big smile. She came up and hugged them both.

The three of them chuckled and reminisced about how Bridgette and her prior classmates all saw how much Rose and Ethan were so obviously in love. She described how all the romantics in their class were jealous of their flirting, and how it even made a few skeptic students turn the corner towards love as well.

The night drew on as the three of them stood talking and traveling down memory lane. But one thing permeated Ethan's mind. He was going to be a father. He was now going to create something besides a painting.

The ambiance of The Rose painting right next to them pulsed in his mind as he thought about the new creation he was making with his wife. With his most significant painting being hung in Bridgette's hall, there was now only one option for Ethan.

Ethan interrupted Bridgette mid-sentence, having obviously been distracted from their conversation due to his unwavering thoughts. "Sorry, Bridgette – is Mr. Olsen's painting for sale?"

Bridgette was caught off guard, knowing it was really Ethan's but also having been informed about his ruse. So she played it cautious by continuing to play along. "I ... uh ... I think Mr. Olsen would only have it be sold to someone who would truly appreciate it."

"Oh, that'd be us!" Rose chimed in, to Ethan's joy.

Bridgette eyed Ethan to read the situation. "Well, it would be an honor then."

"Great," Ethan said. "How much?"

Bridgette had to work hard not to laugh out loud. Her old instructor was now asking her how much it would cost him to buy his own painting – one which he voluntarily gave to her to hang in her hall. Bridgette smiled at the question, and saw Ethan smiling back – knowing he too was finding amusement in the situation.

"I'm serious, how much?" Ethan pressed.

"Well, I'm close with Mr. Olsen. And he said that if I found a buyer that was truly moved by it, then it was theirs for free…"

"No," Rose quickly retorted, "that's not right. A painting like this. I mean – I couldn't have it hanging in our house and living with the guilt of taking it for free."

"That's true," Ethan agreed, finding humor in his wife's ironic statement. "So, Bridgette – what's the price then?"

Bridgette was speechless, feeling cornered by the situation. "I … uh … well, if that's the case. I'm sure Mr. Olsen would be flattered to have the great Ethan Cooley name his own price – to have you name your own value of his finest work." Bridgette's strategic response was both flattering and a funny way to get back at him for putting her in the unexpected and awkward situation.

But both Ethan and Bridgette were surprised to hear Rose blurt out a price. And it was not a modest price, either. Though Rose was aware of their financially-secure means, the price she named still made The Rose easily Bridgette's most expensive piece she would sell.

Ethan didn't balk or even blink at the price. "Deal," he agreed with his wife.

As Bridgette carefully took the painting down and wrapped it for them, Ethan leaned in to his former student. "And the commission's all yours. You have a wonderful gallery – you've earned it."

The two young and expecting lovers departed from the gallery. Rose carefully held the wrapped frame containing The Rose painting, as though she was practicing holding her newborn infant.

"What made you want to buy it?" She asked Ethan as they drove back.

Ethan's tone cracked in honesty as he spoke. "On the same night, I saw my wife wearing the most beautiful dress as she stared at the most beautiful painting and shared the most beautiful news to me. I had to keep these memories together."

"Can we hang it in our house instead of your gallery?" Rose asked.

"Absolutely."

Ethan and Rose drove off into the night, not just excited at the creation which they now owned, but undeniably excited about the new creation which they looked forward to holding in their arms one day.

Chapter 11

"Three – Two – One – Push!" The nurse called out. Below the nurse laid Rose, in the pain of an intense labor. Ethan held her hand, sitting at her side but unsure of if he was actually being any assistance to his wife.

The years passed by swiftly since the day he first found out that he would be a father. Now, about eight years and two children later, the words "father" and "dad" brought about mixed reactions from him. Often times he'd hear his two other children – both daughters – cry out those words in pleas to avoid bedtime. As they grew older, those words would sometimes be said lovingly, though other times they were said in a defiant battle over seemingly meaningless controversies. His oldest was now seven and his other daughter was five years old. But even through the sometimes-constant use of the word "dad," he never took his role as a father for granted. It was a calling in life which he held close to his purpose of living.

Ethan sat by his wife's side, watching her constant pain seem unending through each contraction. Her willingness to endure through each labor reminded Ethan of just how nervous Rose was almost eight years ago when she first revealed to him that she was pregnant with their first child. That nervousness would eventually transform into endlessly being tired, sometimes being frustrated, and never-ending worry about at all of the myriad of small decisions that Rose made on a daily basis as the mother – worrying whether each of those small decisions were in their children's best interests. The nervousness which Rose had that evening almost eight years ago was far eclipsed by the multitude of parental feelings which manifested in the years since.

But now, Ethan was nervous. This child would be his third. But it was also his first son. It wasn't that he wanted a son more than a daughter. That didn't matter so much to him. It was just that he was used to being the father to daughters. Now, he would have a son. It was just different to him. He didn't know if it would actually *be* different than having daughters – but that's what made him so nervous. The fact that he didn't know so much made him nervous. Would he be the fatherly example to his son that he should be? Would he keep him on the right track to one day make his place in the world? Such a wide array of questions and worries ran through Ethan's mind as his wife pushed hard at his side.

"I see his head." The nurse calmly said. Her calmness sent Ethan through the roof. How could she be so calm about what was happening and with how much pain Rose was in? He breathed for a second, telling himself he was having an emotional high.

"I think you have just one more push and you'll be meeting your new baby boy!" The nurse happily said.

"You got this, babe," Ethan tried to motivate Rose. She looked him in the eyes, pain being easily depicted in her glance. But through the pain was perseverance. The perseverance of a mother. And in this moment, pain and perseverance equaled love. Ethan saw this.

He quickly kissed her on the forehead before moving from her side to watch his first son be born at the end of the bed.

Each of his children's births were emotional for him, and this time was no different. As he got up to go to the end of the bed, tears flooded his eyes. He thought of the name which they had mutually arrived at for their son, and the tears began flowing like waterfalls down his cheeks.

When he heard the first cry of his newborn son, Ethan

wiped away the tears, trying to focus on his boy who the nurse was holding.

He kept wiping his eyes, trying to remove the fog of the tears from the center of his vision. But nothing was working. What was going on, he wondered? In the middle of the eyesight in both of his eyes was a hazy fog that covered up the detail from his vision.

Confused about the sudden, unexpected event, Ethan asked the nurse: "Does he need cleaned off?" As he tried to focus on the face of his first son, but couldn't see the detail behind the fog, he hoped that the baby just needed to be cleaned.

"We will in a few – just like every other baby. Would you like to hold him for just a moment before we give him to your wife?" The nurse answered.

"Yes, please."

Ethan held his son in his arms but was unable to get any clarity on his face. His confusion ran rampant and felt insurmountable. What was happening? Holding his son in one arm, he kept trying to wipe his eyes, hoping that his vision would clear up.

"Are you okay, Honey?" Rose asked him from her bed.

"Yes, it's just – he's so beautiful." He said, not wanting to ruin the moment by turning the attention to his eyesight issue.

"Can I see him?" Rose asked, still exhausted from the difficult labor.

Ethan struggled to walk just the few steps to his wife, trying to make sure he wouldn't trip on something while holding the baby. He couldn't make out any detail in the center of his vision of whatever he looked directly at.

Only when he handed their son off to Rose did he realize that his peripheral vision was unchanged. He could clearly see everything in his peripheral vison, such as Rose holding their baby boy.

"Oh look at him, Ethan – he looks just like you!" Rose exclaimed.

From his periphery, Ethan could see that Rose was running her fingers in some of the boy's hair while nursing him. So, Ethan covered up his sight issues by using that info. "I think he looks like you. I mean, look at that hair!" He tried to compliment, hoping that it looked like red hair so that his comment would sound right.

"You're right – I do see some red hair in there. Looks like you'll now have a full family of redheads. Everyone but you."

Rose started running her fingers down along the baby's face while finishing up nursing him. "But his face still looks just like you."

Ethan leaned over Rose's bedside, looking toward the other side of the bed, trying hard to put them in his peripheral vision so that he could see any detail on his son's face better. It was working, too. It took some effort to focus on his peripheral vision instead of the center of his vision. But eventually the face of his newborn son was seen.

"Are you okay?" Rose asked, noticing him staring off to her other side instead of looking straight at them.

Ethan balked, not knowing how to react. She'd noticed his unusual technique. Still not wanting to change the subject away from their new baby, he found an excuse.

He looked straight back at his wife and baby while answering. "Yeah – I just was thinking about how much Lily and Violet will be thrilled to have a new baby in the house."

"Especially a boy!" Rose said. Ethan assumed that she was smiling, but he couldn't see her reaction. If whatever was happening was going to linger in his eyesight for some time, he knew he'd have to listen to the intonations in her voice more closely to see how to react.

Luckily, this time, he was saved by the nurse. "Okay, Rose – I think it's time to give him his first bath. Is his dad going to come along to help, so that mother can rest?"

"You should go," prodded Rose. Ethan had always helped give his other children their first bath and looked forward to it as the only real moment he'd have with his new children before the hospital, mom, and visitors took all of the baby's attention.

"Sure, I'd love to." He said. Ethan stood up to walk to the doorway, but felt uneasy on his feet. He had not yet gotten used to focusing on the ground by looking straight ahead. But when he kicked the end of a table right in front of him, he quickly realized that his way of watching where he was walking would have to change. He also quickly realized that an excuse needed to be given to his wife and the nurse.

"Wow – headrush. I must have gotten up too quickly."

Rose was too exhausted to respond. As soon as Ethan reached the doorway, it sounded like Rose's head hit the pillow, getting some much-needed and much-deserved rest.

Once outside in the hallway, Ethan shut the door to their hospital room. "Nurse, is there a vision center in this hospital?"

"Are you okay, Mr. Cooley?"

"I'm fine – I'm fine. I just think I lost a contact earlier or something."

"Okay. Well the vision center is down the hall and to the right. You should be able to spot it easy."

Ha – funny, Ethan thought. Should be easy to spot the vision center. This nurse must have a cruel sense of humor.

"Do you want me to take your baby to be bathed without you, then?"

"That'd be so nice. I'm sorry. I really need to head down to the vision center." But before the nurse left, Ethan asked one last thing of her. "Oh, but would you do me a favor and not mention any of this to my wife? That was a hard labor, and I don't want to worry her any."

Finding his way to the vision center was no easy task. But it allowed him to practice walking while focusing on his peripheral vision. He didn't know how long he would keep up the ruse up of not telling Rose, but he knew that he had some serious adapting to do in the meantime. And this walk was the perfect opportunity. He didn't exactly master it, but eventually he got the hang of what would be required until the situation got fixed. He didn't know when or how this issue would get fixed, but he knew that it would. After all, he was a painter and an art gallery owner. Eyesight was the most essential of his senses.

"You have macular degeneration." The ophthalmologist said plainly, as if those words would mean something to Ethan.

But they didn't. Ethan always said that he would rather doctors be smart instead of having good bedside manners, but this guy was pushing that perspective out of the window.

"And so, when does that go away?"

"It doesn't."

Ethan paused, trying to take in this horrible news. He just couldn't process it.

"But it just randomly started – can't it just go away, doctor? I can't see a thing in the middle of my vision."

"It doesn't go away, Ethan. I'm sorry."

"Surgery? Can that help?"

"It can slow it, but you're never going to be able to have your vision return to normal."

The doctor's tone was unemotional and matter-of-fact, leading Ethan to almost erupt at the man. But he didn't. Instead, Ethan held it in, trying to process what the man was saying.

"I … uh … medication?"

"There's no medication, Ethan. The nerves leading to your retinas are permanently damaged, they ..."

"That can't happen! I'm a painter – an artist, you know! I can't live without being able to see in the middle of my vision!"

For as bad as the doctor was with his bedside manner, he warmed up a little. "Ethan. I have some worse news for you."

Ethan was sitting on the table in the doctor's office with his legs hanging off of the side. He grabbed hold of his knees to brace for impact.

"You will eventually lose *all* of your eyesight."

The sentence hit him like a bag of bricks fell on his head. So much so, in fact, that Ethan nearly fainted, but still somehow sat on the examination table. He moved his hands up to his face, covering them in despair. Tears began streaming down the sides of his cheeks and onto the cheap pull-out paper that lined the table.

Through his hands, he asked: "How long do I have until I lose it all?"

The doctor hemmed and hawed, letting Ethan know there was very little certainty in his answer. "It varies. Sometimes it's months, and sometimes its years." The doctor paused to think before continuing. "You know, if you're worried about your work, this type of thing should get you on permanent disability from here on out." The doctor wrote something on a pad and handed it to Ethan. "Here, this note should help with that."

Ethan snatched the note before storming over to the door. For as mad as he was at the horrific news, he was just as mad at the classless and impersonal way in which the doctor had approached the very serious issue.

He stormed out of the office and back down the hospital hallway, stumbling from his delirious state of despair as well as not yet perfecting the new way he'd have to see while walking.

His head swirled in the chaos and questions that piled up in his mind. As if to compensate for his vision deficit, his artistic mind turned the hallway into the swirling chaos of an impressionist painting. The Scream. In Ethan's mind, the hospital hallway turned dark like the scene in that famous painting, and Ethan felt like the man screaming in the middle. He now understood how Edvard Munch had been able to paint that screaming man all those years ago. Something terrible had happened to that artist. Just as Ethan created The Rose from a glimpse of the hope that comes from the timelessness of love, Ethan now suspected that Edvard Munch had created The Scream from the hopeless observation of unending misery.

If Ethan had a canvas and oils in front of him, he could easily paint a masterpiece of impressionist gloom rivaling The Scream – one which even Eugene would have appreciated in all of his stoic optimism. But there was no canvas, and Ethan did not have any paints or oils. This was reality. And, for really the first time in his life, Ethan was left to have to deal with reality without being able to run to the crutch of his studio.

Ethan stood outside of his wife's hospital room breathing hard from the despair he felt. Patience and perseverance, he told himself over and over in his mind. He knew he would tell Rose eventually – just not yet. It was still too much for him to process and to put it on a new mother.

He opened the door smiling, putting on a show. He was lucky to have heard a baby sound as soon as he stepped inside, so he knew that Rose was holding their child.

"And how's the perfect little man and mommy doing?" Ethan asked. He went and sat next to his family.

Rose remained silent, leaving him worrying if the nurse had divulged his vision issue to her. He tried to focus on his periphery to see what was going on, but Rose's delayed response calmed his nerves.

"He's just so perfect – like his father." She said in an

appreciative, serious tone. She then moved her hand up to brush Ethan's cheek. "How was your walk?" She asked.

"Good – I just needed to get out for a moment." He made that up. Recalling a bush of roses outside the hospital that they passed by on their way into the hospital, Ethan continued: "There was a small grove of rose bushes that I went to see outside. You know how I love a beautiful rose." He said, half-jokingly but also in a serious tone.

Rose's attention turned back to their newborn son. "I'm glad we have a son – I'm glad *you* have a son, now." Ethan could tell that Rose was again brushing her fingers along the baby's cheek as she held him.

Rose kept talking while she brushed the cheek of their new son. "And I think his name is perfect."

The gravity of the statement caught Ethan off guard, instantly filling his eyes with tears. He sniffled and cleared his throat before responding. "Yeah. I think it's perfect too."

"He would have been so happy with who you've become," Rose continued lovingly, "I think Eugene is the perfect name for our son."

Chapter 12

"Hold still, almost done." Ethan said while putting the last touches on his newest painting.

"C'mon, dad – I'm getting tired." Complained Violet. "I've been sitting still for an hour."

"I know, girly, but I'm so close. Just a few more minutes - *please.*"

In the final moments of her patience, the six-year-old noticed something about her dad which she hadn't noticed in the hour that she'd held still.

"Dad, you look funny when you paint." She remarked bluntly. "Why do you do that?"

"Do what?" He asked while still fixated on the final strokes of his daughter's portrait.

"You don't actually look at me or the canvas – you, I dunno – you look to the side." Again with the bluntness that only a young child could have, Violet remarked: "You look funny."

It'd been a year since Ethan discovered his handicap. In

that year, he'd pressed on with two things.

First, he learned to compensate for the lack of direct vision by using his peripheral vision even more. He'd become so natural at this that he often even forgot that he was looking to the side. But still, as each month passed by, the cloudy haze in the middle of his eyesight slightly expanded. He knew he had to accelerate the speed in which he painted his family members if he was going to reach the desperate goal he set for himself. It's due to this desperatation that he pleaded for his young daughter to sit still for just a few moments longer.

The second thing which Ethan pressed on with during the last year was something that he was admittedly ashamed of. He persisted with not divulging his blindness to his family – and it especially pained him to keep it from Rose. But the longer that he went without revealing his handicap, the longer that he felt like it was somehow okay. He knew it wasn't. Some days his limitations wore so frustratingly heavy on him that he wanted to blurt it out to Rose the moment he saw her. But he never did. Perhaps it was because he knew the weight of the burden and sought – through love – to not place that weight upon his family. Perhaps it was because he felt that the longer it went without him telling Rose, the more likely he wasn't just revealing his blindness but also his lie – as though the issue had compounded and he didn't have the guts to reveal it all. Or perhaps it was simply because Ethan was embarrassed. Ashamed. And he was. Deeply.

He knew it wasn't his fault that he had begun to lose his vision. But he still did. He was an artist without the ability to see. He was also an art connoisseur and gallery owner without the ability to see the art that hung on his walls. Without his art, he often felt as though he had nothing. And without his sight, he could not have his art. So, to admit that he could not see was – to Ethan – to admit that he no longer had anything.

Ethan knew that, in reality, he had something – he had his family. But it was still a tough transition to make away from the world of painting, when that was all he could ever remember wanting to do in life.

So, for those many reasons, Ethan felt reluctantly compelled to persist with his lie.

"I look funny, huh?" Ethan's tone was mocking, trying to make a joke to detract his middle daughter's attention away from the answer to her question. "You wanna make fun of the guy who's painting your picture? Oh … that's a dangerous thing to do!" Violet chuckled at her dad's joke. "I mean, what if I make you cross eyed or something and then hang it by the front door for everyone to see?"

"Dad …"

"And I'd call it Ms. Cross-Eyed." Ethan was now using his wife's inclination to make up nicknames as a way to tease someone.

"Dad … don't! I mean it."

With one final touch of his paintbrush to the canvas, Ethan sidestepped away from his joking by turning serious. "There – done! Come on over and tell me what you think."

The young girl hopped down from the pedal stool and walked over to see the painting which her father had worked on for the last several weeks. Every Wednesday after school, her mom would drop her off at her dad's studio, where she sat as patiently as she could for her father to paint her portrait. She didn't know why he was so persistent in wanting to paint portraits of their whole family, and she wasn't really sure that she wanted to sit as long as it would take. This was why she held out to be the last of her siblings to have her portrait be painted. She saw how long it took for her sister Lily and her younger brother Eugene to have theirs done. Violet seriously doubted that she wanted to remain still for so long. But her dad insisted. And like her mom always did, her mom supported him.

But now, after reluctantly sitting so still for what seemed like an eternity to the young girl, Violet got to see her finished portrait for the first time.

And just like a six-year-old will do, her bluntness reigned supreme. "I don't like it," she said with her nose curled up.

"You don't like it?" Her father repeated in surprise.

"Yeah, I mean – I think it's ugly."

Something didn't seem right to Ethan, though. He caught on to what Violet was really saying. "What's so ugly about it?"

"Well, I don't like the red hair. It's … different than other people's hair. I think the kids at school would call it ugly."

There it was. The honesty of his daughter's self-depreciating words cut through Ethan straight to the core.

He kneeled down close to his daughter to be on her level. "I think it's beautiful. In fact, don't tell your sister and brother – but this one is my favorite."

"Yeah, but you gave me red hair."

"Well, girly, you have red hair. And it's beautiful just like your mother's. Did I ever tell you that your mom's red hair was the first thing that I …"

"I don't like it!" She stubbornly interrupted.

Ethan paused for a moment. Patience and perseverance, he told himself.

"Here, I wanna show you something that I've never showed anyone else, okay?" He said calmly. "But if I show it to you, you have to promise not to tell anyone else – can you do that for me?"

Violet nodded in hesitation, not sure what she was getting herself into. Ethan held her in one arm and lifted her up to the height of the canvas.

The paint had now dried enough for him to place his hand on it lightly without ruining the detail of the painting. Though this was the first time that he was feeling the brushstrokes of the painting in front of any of his family members, he was very well acquainted with doing this in secret over the last several months.

Ethan placed his fingers carefully on the painting and closed his eyes. He carefully traced the feeling of the brushstrokes while holding Violet in his other arm.

"What are you doing, daddy?" She asked, not knowing what was happening in front of her.

Ethan opened his eyes. "Remember you promised, okay?

Don't tell anyone."

Violet nodded eagerly, interested to see what her dad was talking about. Ethan held his daughter's hand up to his painting carefully. Extending her pointer finger, he placed it on the painting.

"Okay, now close your eyes."

"What for?"

"You'll see."

The young girl closed her eyes, with her finger still touching the contours of the brushstrokes. Ethan moved her finger around the painting while he described aloud what part of the painting she was feeling with her eyes closed.

"This is the outline of your face," her dad said while Violet's eyes remained closed. "Can you feel the shape of your face?"

Violet was startled – she could! As her dad traced the outline of her face in the painting with her finger, the image appeared in her mind. Instinctively she opened up her palm and outstretched her other fingers.

Ethan moved the young girl's fingers around the other parts of her face.

"I intentionally used thick paint so that I can feel your

face with my eyes … closed." He was careful not to divulge the real reason for using the thick paints due to his blindness.

He continued describing almost every detail he would feel in the painting, as his daughter remained captivated. "Feel this? This is your mouth – it's smiling, isn't it? Feel the smile?"

Violet nodded. She not only felt it, but the image of it appeared in her mind as her eyes were still closed.

"And feel your eyes? These are your eyes," he said while moving her fingers around them. "Do you feel how they also almost have a way of smiling?"

Violet chuckled, assuming her dad was making a joke.

"I mean," he continued, "not smiling like your mouth, but just also … happy. Even though your eyes are closed now as you feel the brushstrokes, you can almost feel the light that's inside your eyes within the painting."

Violet didn't really know what her dad was talking about – but the strange thing was, she somehow felt it. In her mind were her eyes, and they stood out as if they were smiling and filled with light.

"What do you see?" Her father asked.

"I see it!" She smiled. "I really do – it's like I'm happy to see you or something."

This description made Ethan smirk. "Yes, I've seen that look on your face many times. It's kinda what I was going for when I painted it. Isn't it beautiful – aren't *you* beautiful?"

Violet nodded. The new image in Violet's mind had made her forget about her earlier statement that she thought she was ugly. But Ethan hadn't forgot it – not at all.

"Okay, what am I tracing now?" He asked as he moved her outstretched fingers around the outline of her hair.

"Oh, that's my hair! I can tell easy."

"What does it make you see in your mind, Violet?"

"… nothing … yet."

Ethan retraced her hair with her fingers, and kept doing so until her mind painted its own picture.

"I see it!" She suddenly exclaimed.

"See what?"

"I see my hair."

"And isn't it just as beautiful as your smiling eyes and mouth?"

"It is! Oh – wow, I see it now. And I feel it too."

"You can open your eyes now, Violet."

Violet's green eyes stared into her father's eyes. "Violet, you *are* beautiful. Everything about you. I need you to know that."

Violet reluctantly nodded her head, now remembering what she initially said about the painting.

"Violet, I need you to know that that's why I painted you. Because you're beautiful and I never ever want to forget it. I love how your eyes smile just as wide as your happy mouth. And I love your hair – oh, your beautiful hair!"

Violet was listening intently and a smile cracked her mouth, being drawn into her father's compliments.

Ethen continued complimenting his daughter because he wanted her to understand exactly what he saw – while he was still able to actually see it. "Did you know that you have hair just like your mom's? I don't think I ever told you – but it was her red hair that stood out to me the most when I saw her for the first time. I thought that her brilliant, wavy red hair was so gorgeous that I had to go talk to her. And I'm glad I did because now I have you – and you look just as beautiful as your mom."

Instinctively, Violet leaned in and hugged her dad. While pulled in close, Ethan said aloud into her ear. "And never forget it – because I never want to forget it. Promise?"

"Promise." Young Violet said. But it's what she said next

that surprised Ethan. "And dad, you're very handsome too. I'll never forget that – even if I go blind one day."

Violet's last words immediately startled Ethan, sending a tear down his cheek as he continued to hug his daughter. "I promise, too – I'll never forget how beautiful you are Violet, even if I go blind one day."

Chapter 13

"C'mon – let's go see if your mom is outside," Ethan said calmly to Violet, allowing the personal moment between them to end. "She should be here by now to pick us up."

Since Ethan discovered that his vision loss would be imminent, he reserved each Wednesday night to have one-on-one time with each of his children. They'd come into his studio to be painted by Ethan, and Ethan certainly enjoyed memorializing them into a painting. Of course, the intent of those paintings was to preserve his memory of their appearance. Just as he'd done with young Violet, Ethan fully intended to remember their faces by tracing the thickness of his paint with his fingers later. This was his backup plan in case his memory failed him with old age and made it so that he struggled to remember what his own children's faces looked like. He'd initially hoped to hold off painting Eugene's portrait last, hoping that his baby would be a little older when he memorialized his countenance. But that just didn't work out. Ethan knew that he didn't have that much time – his vision was fading fast.

Regardless, Ethan soon saw his painting not as a passion but as a blessing to allow him to do what a simple photograph could not – allow him to trace its contours to repaint his children's faces in his mind. He felt fortunate, indeed.

And because the purpose of his paintings was to capture their faces before he lost his eyesight entirely, he was diligent in trying to quickly, but accurately, paint his children. But although he would try and rush the actual painting, what he didn't want to rush were the moments of conversation with his children. He relished these simple moments with them – just father and child. Sometimes, they'd ask him questions about his methods. Sometimes they'd just simply ask him how his day was. Regardless of the question, Ethan would often turn it around and ask his child questions instead. He knew that the sound of their voices is what would eventually be the basis of his relationships with them. That, and he often learned of their own passions and ideas just by simply listening to his young children speak their minds. It was fascinating to Ethan how listening could be a skill just as important as his skills with the paintbrush.

So, Ethan's heart dropped just a bit when he realized his

last formal Wednesday appointment with each of his children had just come to an end because he'd now finished each of their portraits.

But then, an unexpected inquiry from Violet instantly lifted his hopes: "Hey, dad?"

"Yeah…"

"I kinda like seeing your painting of me now. Do you think you could teach me a little about painting? Maybe I could come back next Wednesday?"

Bingo. Ethan was about to immediately jump at saying yes when he was surprised by the sound of his wife's voice from behind them.

"You want to learn to paint, huh? Watch out – once you open that door, there's no closing it." Rose taunted them both. She walked up behind her husband and pecked him on the cheek before looking ahead at Violet's finished portrait. "Looks great, you two! Now, when's my portrait going to happen?"

Ethan smiled at his wife's welcomed taunting. "Well, maybe tonight if you play your cards right," Ethan tried to flirt. He may have gotten better with words since meeting Rose all those years back, but one thing was still for sure. Of the both of them, Rose was still way better at flirting than he would ever be.

"What if I said that it was *you* who had to play your cards right?" Just the playful tone of her voice put Ethan's flirting to shame. Above it all, though, they both had fun flirting in front of a completely clueless six-year-old, who probably thought her parents were talking about playing a real card game.

Rose changed the subject, though. "Oh! We have to get going. I told my parents that I'd be by to drop off their mail that I collected while they were out of town last week."

Ethan wasn't thrilled to hear this due to the long-lingering rift that existed between him and his in-laws, and it showed in his tone. "… You didn't tell them I was coming by also, did you?" Ethan intentionally asked the question as a leading question, hoping it'd get him out of an impromptu visit with Rose's father.

"No, don't worry. I told them it would just be a quick drop-by to give them the mail."

Ethan froze. Now he was worried. Whereas he should be thrilled he didn't have to see his in-laws tonight, that was no longer on his mind. He was going to be driving his wife and children in the car at night. This couldn't happen.

It'd been about a year since his vision loss had manifested. But in that year, he'd worked so hard to make his lack of driving become a casual thing. Luckily, they didn't live that far away from his studio. In fact, it was really only a couple minutes' drive from their upscale suburb neighborhood just on the edge of downtown. On the days with good weather, he would instead walk – choosing to risk his own health from walking on the sidewalk for about thirty minutes instead of going behind the wheel.

Even then, the vast majority of days, he used public transportation. He'd told his family that he preferred this for environmental concerns and because being out in the public helped him find creative inspiration. But those were just excuses to hide the fact that he was trying to avoid driving due to his poor vision. Even when he was absolutely unable to avoid driving the handful of times in the last year, his driving had been during the daylight and without anyone else in the car. This was much different.

Ethan began to fret internally, trying to think of anyway to casually get out of the situation.

"You know, Honey – why don't you drive tonight?" He asked casually as the three of them left his studio and walked out onto the sidewalk.

"Ethan, can you please drive? I have a headache, and I'm

not even at my parent's house yet. I now have to think of an excuse for why we're not staying to eat dinner with them tonight– since I actually had told them we'd all stay to eat. You know, one of these days, things between you and my father are going to erupt. You really should try to see things from his perspective. I'm his only daughter, so he's over-protective of me."

"Tell me about it," Ethan mumbled to himself.

"What was that?" Rose asked, not having heard what he said.

"Where are Lilly and Eugene?" Ethan changed the subject. He was still trying to think of anything that he could to find an excuse not to drive. Maybe this issue would help somehow.

"Oh, yeah – they're being watched by the neighbors. We need to pick them up once we get home. That's actually a good reason for us not to stay at my parents – I'll just say we have to go pick up our other kids."

Nothing. Ethan couldn't think of a single thing to help him get out of the situation. And Rose obviously didn't notice his motivation to get out of driving, since she was so caught up in the change of plans with her parents.

Ethan was stuck. It was either tell the truth at this random, sporadic moment, or do the best he could to drive at night.

He hated himself as he got into the front driver seat and turned on the car. As front headlights flicked on, he despised that he didn't have enough courage to end his lie. It gnawed and clawed at him, making him promise himself internally that he would soon tell his wife what he was going through. But that was a moment which Ethan wanted to control, not being cornered into it by the circumstance of being asked to drive home at night. Besides, he figured it was evening - so there would be less cars on the road.

"Everyone have their seatbelts on?" He asked casually. Nods were given in response. "It's been so long since I've actually had to drive. Are you sure you don't wanna drive?" Ethan continued. "You could just drop us off at home and then stay for dinner at your parent's."

"No, I'm fine. They've been on vacation. All they'll want to do is talk about it, and I just have a splitting headache."

Ethan spurred on conversation with Rose while he drove, using it as a reason to turn his head more frequently to make it appear like he was looking at her. When he would do that, he could much more easily use his peripheral vision to see the road ahead.

"You know, babe," Rose said, "I'm glad you cut down your art classes to just the high school class. I'm glad that it's let you focus more on the gallery and your painting instead."

But before Ethan could say anything back, Violet's interruption left Ethan scrambling for another excuse.

"Yeah, but mom – dad looks funny these days when he's painting."

"Funny, huh?" Ethan joked. "Be nice, now. Remember what I said – if you make fun of me, I'll make you look funny the next time I paint you!" Ethan tried to change the subject back to what Rose had said about his teaching classes. "But, yeah – I think teaching just began to wear on me over the years."

But Rose wasn't having any of it. "Wait a minute – he looks funny, huh?" She asked Violet in the back seat. "I mean I always knew he looked funny in general, but what are you talking about?"

Ethan glanced to the side, staring at his wife. He was both simultaneously trying to focus on the road in his peripheral vision while reading what little he could of his wife's reaction through the haze of his central vision.

"Well, daddy just likes to look to the side a lot while painting. That's all." Violet remarked.

"What, kinda like he's doing now?" Rose asked Violet as she looked back at Violet. The tone of her voice was as if she was mockingly playing with her husband. But still, Ethan's heart was beating like a drum in his chest. They were so close to discovering his vision deficiency that Ethan did the only thing he could think of to cover it up. He looked straight ahead.

With the cloud of his visual degeneration now staring straight ahead, he never even saw it. Everything instantly changed in the erupting sound of a loud crash – the road, their ride home, and his life. All changed forever.

The next several moments were as blurry as his vision.

He awoke, to the swirling chaos around him. He heard an ambulance in the distance and felt that their car was tipped on its side. The sting of broken shards of glass radiated on his face. As he reached up to wipe the glass from off of him, he felt the cold wetness of a line of blood. He was lying on his left side, strapped in by his seat belt, which told him that his car had tipped over so that his side of the car was against the asphalt.

In panic, he looked all around, trying hard to see anything

that would tell him he was okay.

"Rose?" He yelled out loud. "Violet?" His cloudy vision prevented him from seeing if they were okay, leaving him in fear that his lie had taken from him the only thing that truly mattered in life. His family.

He heard coughing from the back seat.

"Violet, is that you? Are you alright?" He asked frantically.

"I'm okay," the faint voice of the six-year-old said from behind him. But the faintness of that voice still left him worried. Even more concerning was that he hadn't heard from Rose yet.

He tried hard to focus his peripheral eyesight and was alarmed to find her hanging down through the middle of the car just inches from him – hanging from the seatbelt. She wasn't moving.

"Rose – Honey." Ethan said as he quickly moved his arm to tap her on the shoulder. "Babe – are you okay? Talk to me." Ethan's eyesight rapidly became worse as tears filled his eyes, leaving him unable to see if there was any reaction from the woman he knew he loved from the moment he saw her. "Rose, are you okay? Rose, wake up!"

"Ethan, I'm here – I'm okay. I'm staring right at you." She said calmly, though pain was heard in her voice.

Ethan's heart dropped. He had done this to the only love of his life, and he couldn't even see if she was okay.

"What happened?" He asked through the tears flowing down his cheeks.

"You hit a pole on the side of the road." Rose said.

Ethan's tears intensified. "I'm sorry – I'm *so* sorry."

Despite hanging down through the middle of the car suspended by her seatbelt, Rose managed to move her arm to touch her husband's cheek. "We're alright, Ethan. It's okay."

Still, Ethan could do nothing else besides let the remorse of his actions – his long-held lie – seep out through his tears.

Even in this most dreadful and physically-painful moment, Rose was an angel. She had every reason to react in anger from what happened. Yet, she didn't. Just as she always did, she tried to lighten up her ailing husband. "Violet, you're alright, right?" Rose asked to the back of the car where Violet was laying on her side but otherwise did not appear injured.

"I'm alright … daddy, don't cry."

Ethan had enough. "I can't see you," he said through his continued crying.

But neither Rose nor Violet understood the true meaning of what he just admitted aloud.

"I know daddy, but I'm back here. I had my seat belt on, so I'm okay – just like you and mommy."

Rose continued to caress Ethan's cheek as he laid sobbing beneath Rose's dangling body.

"No," he said, "I mean …"

But suddenly the top car door next to Rose was pried open, preventing him from explaining what he really meant.

"Are you all okay in there?" A voice asked.

Rose took the lead, "We're okay. Just need some help getting out."

Ethan heard the firefighters first extricate Rose.

"Mam, I think you have a broken collar bone. We need to transport you to the hospital right away."

The firefighter's news tore through Ethan like a fire would tear through a piece of paper. Rose's angelic attempt to calm him was a coverup of how much pain she'd actually been in, and now he knew it. He'd hurt her, yet in that moment of pain she still sought to take care of him. Deep feelings of worthlessness and being undeserving of her tore him into pieces.

When the firefighter next reached to free him, Ethan was insistent: "No – help my daughter next. I'm fine."

Violet's faint coughing from the back seat summoned great fear in Ethan that he'd hurt his little girl. The only thing he had to do in life was protect her, and he feared that he had let her down in the arrogance and selfishness of his lie.

"Girly – you still okay back there ... Violet?" His voice trembled as he asked.

Another faint cough was heard before his daughter's voice answered back up. "Yeah, daddy. I'm okay."

Ethan's worse fears were calmed when he heard the firefighter reassure Violet. "Yep, I think you got lucky. I don't even see a cut on you."

"She's coughing, though ..." Ethan asked concerned.

"I think it just surprised me, dad."

"I think you're probably right," agreed the firefighter. "Just to be safe, though – wanna ride in the ambulance with your mom? We can double check at the hospital to make sure you're okay, even though I think you're fine."

"Yeah!" The girl excitedly replied. Ethan was thrilled to hear her excitement as she no longer seemed to be faint.

"Okay, just your daddy is left."

With the firefighter extricating him, Ethan asked. "Are you sure she's okay? Or were you just saying that to calm her down?"

"Oh, I don't think she's calm right now," joked the fireman. "She's as excited as can be about her first ride in an ambulance. She'll be just fine."

Ethan's seatbelt was cut, allowing him to stand up inside the car. After being helped outside of it, the firefighter asked him: "How about you? Do you feel any pain?"

Ethan wanted to respond that he felt the pain of his lie – that the cold feeling of letting his family down was the worse pain he ever could imagine. But he didn't. "No, I think I'm fine. Just a few scratches is all."

"Well, your wife and daughter are about to head to the hospital in that ambulance. We'll take you there separately after we get some info from you."

Ethan stood next to his demolished car – its trashed state mirroring how trashed he felt inside. He watched as the ambulance pulled away - the blaring red lights signaling to him that his life needed to change. What the ambulance held inside of it was all that mattered to him. His family. They mattered more than his lie. They mattered more than his vision. They mattered more than his painting. They were everything to him, and he knew what he had to do.

Chapter 14

Ethan paced the hallway of the hospital, thinking about nothing besides how he wanted to finally reveal his blindness to Rose. Unfortunately, they had taken her to get scans of her collarbone fracture, and Ethan knew that he couldn't just jump on her with the serious news immediately.

Indeed, he knew that the conversation would have to wait once he saw Rose be carted back from the scanning and down the hallway into a room. She was fast asleep.

Ethan quickly walked down the hall and entered her dark room. Not wanting to wake her up, he quietly pulled a chair to her side. A tear welled up in his eye as he thought about finally divulging his long-held secret to Rose. Delicately, he moved a piece of her curly red hair from in front of her face. She was even more beautiful now than the day he met her. All the ups and downs they'd been through in the years since that defining moment when they met so many years ago had only made her beauty resonate even brighter. Even though he had a hard time seeing her now through the shadows of his hazy vision, that shadowing contained incredible beauty.

But as he sat next to her bedside while she slept, Ethan worried about how Rose would react to what he needed to tell her. He knew that she'd handle it as perfectly as she always handled everything. But still, he worried. He worried that she might think less of him. He worried that she might feel overburdened with now having to take care of him in addition to three young children. He worried that she'd feel betrayed that he kept a secret from her for so long. He worried that she'd feel sorry for him. He worried that she would be concerned with their financial abilities, even though she really had no reason to. He worried about these things and so much more – these were the type of worries that held him back in the past from divulging what he knew he had to tell her.

But not today. It was time. Even though he worried about the effect it would have on her, he knew she was strong. The first time he met Rose, she stood as firm and grounded as a real rose in the wind. And since then, her roots have only gotten more firm. That was among the things he loved about her.

Then a knock came from the hospital door. Ethan stood to go answer it, figuring that it was time for a doctor to check-up on Rose – or maybe even to reveal the outcome of her xrays.

The hospital room lights stayed off as Ethan opened the door. The haze of his vision blocked his view of the doctor at the door, so Ethan just moved out of the way without saying a single word. His expression also remained unmoved, just letting the doctor in to do his check-up.

But Ethan was wrong. Terribly wrong. His assumptions were way off, and he knew it immediately once he heard the voice speak from whom he thought was the doctor.

"Is that it? Not even a hello?" His father-in-law's skeptical voice asked.

"I … no … it's just that …" Ethan scrambled to make an excuse. "I didn't want to wake her up."

Earl entered the hospital room like he owned the place, and his wife Martha followed close behind. Whereas Martha was always much more cordial and welcoming, she often would take the backseat when her husband's disapproval of Ethan was being expressed so blatant. And this was definitely one of those moments.

"Oh, *now* you want to take care of her." Earl's words stung, but unfortunately they weren't the first time he'd been so blunt.

Ethan already knew he was beyond wrong for what he'd done, and he certainly didn't need Earl to remind him of it. Ethan knew he let his wife down, and he also let his daughter down. This wasn't about Earl. Ethan already felt worthless and a failure to his family. So, Earl's skepticism was not met with the normal patience that Ethan always tried to have when talking to his father-in-law.

Earl was used to being able to disparage Ethan without Ethan putting up any verbal fight. So, Ethan's combative response caught Earl by surprise as he walked past Ethan to see his daughter's condition.

"What did you say?" Ethan confronted his father-in-law.

"What? Did I hurt your feelings?" Earl snapped back.

Ethan couldn't see any detail on Earl's face, but he still wasn't going to put up with anything from his unsupportive in-laws. "Apologize, right now, Earl. Be a man."

Martha groaned from the side of Earl, uneasy with the escalation unfolding in front of her.

"Apologize for what? You? You did this to her."

"You know what? That's so like you." Ethan vented.

Through the years, Earl had only become much more vocal about his non-approval of Ethan. In all the years putting up with Earl's unfounded criticism, this was the first time ever that Ethan decided to take a stand. Ethan would even try to take the high road in the past when his father-in-law would criticize him in front of his children.

But not today. Ethan wasn't having any of it. Unfortunately, Ethan learned that Earl would only meet strength with strength — as if he bullied others just to try and raise confrontation. And Ethan learned this for the first time by Earl suddenly whipping around and standing right in front of his face, looking him in the eyes.

"What'd you say to me?" Spit flew from Earl's angry mouth onto Ethan as he said those words — Earl was that close to Ethan's face.

"I said — that's just like you." Ethan didn't have a problem looking the bully in the face, because Ethan couldn't actually see his face. Ethan realized this and felt as though he had the high ground in their argument. What had initially begun as a confrontation stemming from Ethan's inability to see had now turned into an argument that Ethan wasn't afraid of because he couldn't see.

"What's just like me?" Earl said, fuming just inches away from Ethan's face.

"Being a bully."

Ethan's words hung in the air while Earl stewed in front of him. If it was anyone else besides his family – if it was a co-worker from the steel plant – he would have knocked the man out. So, instead, Earl only had his words to fight with.

"You think I'm a bully? Who raised her? I did. And for what? So she could marry you? You don't even do anything. You just paint … like a little wussy."

"Take it back," Ethan warned sternly.

"I ain't taking nothing back."

"Take it back or I swear …" Ethan didn't exactly know what he would threaten against his father-in-law. But he didn't have to, as Martha chimed in.

"Oh, take it back, Earl. Let's just forget about it."

"Take it back? This all started when you hurt my little girl and then didn't even say anything to me when I got to the hospital."

"Just like you – being a bully." Ethan repeated.

"What's going on?" Rose's voice asked in a confused tone as she awoke to the confrontation at the end of her hospital bed. "Dad, what are you doing here?"

"Well, I initially came to see how you and Violet were

doing. But now that I'm here and your husband's being so rude to me …" Earl began. Rose glanced at Ethan like she knew it couldn't really be his fault, but also reminding him to try and take the high road. Earl continued: "… But now that I see what type of man you have to put up with, I've come to take you and your kids home to our house."

"Oh, calm down, dad. I'm not going anywhere."

"But he hurt you – look at you!"

"Dad, you weren't even in the car. Trust me, this was an accident. Besides, it's not even that bad at all – they told me it's barely even a fracture."

Ethan stood listening to his wife stand up for him as she laid in the shadow of his vision. He no longer cared about whatever Earl said. Just hearing his wife support him despite all the mistakes he'd made reinforced how angelic she was. He was deeply and madly in love with the woman, and nothing could change that.

Because of that love, Ethan was willing to do anything. So, right now, he knew what he had to do – not for himself, but because Rose's beautiful confidence in him deserved it.

"Earl, I'm sorry." Ethan said. "I was frustrated. But I'm sure this didn't just startle us, you must have been really worried too once you found out." Ethan didn't really believe a word he was saying, but it didn't matter. Rose deserved the best, and he would give it to her just as she had given it to him just now.

To Ethan's surprise, Earl backed down. Just as he had met confrontation with confrontation, Earl had unexpectedly reacted to an apology with the same thing.

"I'm sorry too, Ethan. I didn't mean what I said."

Martha smiled next to him, glad that the situation diffused without having to take a side.

"But next time, try not to look so indifferent when you see us."

With that, Ethan was reminded of what he really needed to say to his wife. Only, there was no way that he could say it in front of his in-laws.

"Earl, Martha – would you mind giving me a few minutes to talk to Rose alone?"

Though Earl had just apologized, he was hesitant to respond quickly, almost as if he was concerned that Ethan would say bad things about him the moment he left.

Martha picked up on this, though. "Earl, let's go check on Violet. I saw her playing in the children's waiting room with all the toys. I'm sure she'll be thrilled to see us."

For as much as a bully as Earl could be, Ethan had never seen him disparage or even disagree with his wife. This moment was no different.

"Yeah, good idea," Earl said. "We'll be back in a few, Rose. And don't worry – we're not taking any of you home with us." As Earl turned to leave the hospital room, he winked at Ethan after that statement, just like a recovering bully would do to taunt his victim.

Ethan walked over to the door and shut it, leaving just him and Rose alone in the silence of the room. This was the moment. Unlike earlier, he no longer felt nervous.

But Rose could tell from the expression on his face that he had something serious to discuss. "What is it, Ethan?"

Ethan pulled his chair right up to Rose's side on the hospital bed. He placed his hand on her cheek, feeling the contours of her face with his fingertips – just as he would with a painting – to feel her reaction. His thumb was held softly against the corner of her eye, to feel if she was crying or if she was staying strong for him.

This was finally happening. "We need to talk, Rose."

Chapter 15

"Ethan, what's happening?" The tone in Rose's voice was nervous, so Ethan knew he had to cut straight to his point.

"Rose, I'm holding your cheek right now…" But Ethan couldn't finish the sentence as tears streaked down his cheeks. He knew he needed to be strong, but he still had difficulty finding the words. For the first time since he'd met Rose, he again found himself not good with words. As the tears seeped from his eyes, he wished that he could instead paint a picture to express how he felt.

"Rose, I'm holding your cheek right now," he tried again, though his voice was cracking from sadness. He knew now why he was sad. Initially, he was reluctant to tell Rose about his blindness for a myriad of reasons. But now, he knew the real reason. He was terribly and hopelessly saddened by the fact that he could no longer see the most beautiful thing that he'd ever seen in his life. He could no longer see Rose. "Rose – I'm blind."

He felt it. It was small, telling him that she was sad but

also instinctively trying to be strong for her husband. But he felt a tear well up on the side of her eye.

"Blind – like from the accident?" She asked. "I remember you saying that you couldn't see…" Rose searched for answers or, at least, some type of explanation.

Ethan sniffled through his tears. "No, it's been longer than that."

Rose paused for a moment as she retraced her mind to see the clues to what was now unfolding to her. "For how long?"

Ethan loved that her tone was not one of skepticism or anger. Though she'd always been able to be so jokingly lighthearted, she could be serious as the right time. He'd learned that about her from her seriousness at interpreting his paintings, and he saw it again now.

But Ethan felt that his truthful answer only made the tears begin streaming down his love's face. The words didn't come easy to him, but he had to be honest.

"I've never really seen Eugene's face. I noticed it for the first time right as he was born. Instead of seeing his face, I just saw this hazy cloud in the middle of my vision. So instead of bathing him for the first time, I went to see a doctor in this hospital – just down the hall from here, actually. He said I have macular degeneration, and he couldn't tell me when I'd lose my sight completely. But it could be very soon – it's gotten progressively worse the last several months. I'd say it's more than half gone right now, and I only have some of my peripheral vision left."

It all made sense to Rose. She wasn't naïve to how her husband would often look to the side, but she thought it just some type of mannerism he'd developed from years of staring intensely at paintings. This was why she pressed Violet in the car for what her daughter meant by Ethan looking funny while painting. And it all made sense now.

But despite this, one thing stood out to Rose most. "You've never seen Eugene's face?" She barely was able to ask the question without choking up in pity and hurt for her husband.

Ethan just shook his head as he sniffled, trying hard to hold back any more tears.

Through her own tears, Rose said something that meant everything to Ethan. "He's *so* beautiful. He looks just like you. Eugene would be proud of your most beautiful creation."

Ethan didn't know how to react. Rose's words meant that

much to him. So, he did the one thing he always wanted to do. He leaned in and passionately kissed Rose on the lips. He couldn't see her, but he felt her. He felt the softness of her lips on his. Their tears were mixed together, making them one physically, emotionally, and in purpose. Ethan felt the calming and humbling reassurance that Rose would help him despite his inabilities. Rose would continue to love him, and for that he felt not just eternally indebted, but eternally grateful.

In the vast garden of the entire world, he had found the one true rose which stood out as the most beautiful and magnificent of all. And he felt like the luckiest man in the whole world that Rose somehow saw something in him which made her love him back.

Their kiss lingered, as it felt so good to feel Rose. When it broke, Rose didn't yet inject her trademark humor that she often used to make Ethan's seriousness more lighthearted. Instead, she wanted to let Ethan know that she felt compassion for what he'd been going through.

"So that's why you cut your classes down to one?"

"Yeah."

"And that's why you suddenly wanted to paint the children, huh?"

"Yeah, that's why."

"Ethan, that's such a beautiful thing for you to do." Now, Rose's hand had moved to caress his face.

"It wasn't easy." Ethan said, referring to his loss of vision.

Rose knew what Ethan was referring to, but she still found a way to make her husband laugh through the wetness of their tears. "I certainly bet it wasn't easy with Violet! Painting her must have been like trying to paint grasshoppers!"

Ethan chuckled. "Yeah, she was tough, alright."

"And painting Eugene – I mean, you really couldn't tell that he looks like you?" Her tone was joking, which Ethan appreciated. He didn't want his blindness to always be a solemn topic.

"Oh, shoot – I painted him with your eyes. Well, I was just guessing after all." Ethan tried to joke back, but his jokes were never as funny as his wife's.

"Really, Ethan. You could have just felt your face while painting, and then subtract thirty years and two hundred pounds!" Now Rose's jokes were getting kinda cruel, but Ethan appreciated their diversion nonetheless.

"Hey…" Ethan responded, pretending that her joke got to him.

"What, Mr. Magoo – did I hurt your feelings?"

Even though very creative, Rose's reference to the famously ignorant blind cartoon character was somewhat crossing the line. "C'mon, Rose – that's not funny. I'm being serious."

If Ethan could see his wife in front of him, he would have seen that her last joke made her laugh so hard that her slightly-fractured collar bone sent her into spasms of pain. Not even her cast could contain her sense of humor.

But when she calmed down from her painful laughter, she again got serious. "I know you are, Ethan. This is serious. Our lives will never be the same. And that's okay – we will always have each other."

"How will we tell the kids?"

"However you'd like us to. But we'll do it together – just as we've always done everything together and we always will."

"I don't deserve you, Rose."

Rose paused for a moment - thinking before saying another word. "Ethan, would you paint my portrait too? I don't ever want you to forget what I look like."

"I could never forget what you look like."

"I mean it – will you?"

The Sight of Love

"I would love to."

Chapter 16

"Dad, why aren't you driving?" Lilly asked from the rear seat.

"You obviously weren't in the car the last time he drove," Violet said in her unabashedly matter-of-fact tone.

"Yeah, you're right…" Lilly replied, "thanks for driving mom!"

Rose glanced at Ethan sitting in the front seat while chuckling.

"Well, one of you should tell your mom to watch the road," Ethan yelled back jokingly to his kids. "Who knows – a pole might jump out in front of her."

The laughter of their girls rang out from the back sat before Lilly asked: "Where are we going, anyways?"

"Well, your father and I want to take you to where we had our first date a long time ago – Sweet Shop Café!"

"Uh oh," Violet remarked in a sense of dread, "we have to hear stories about their memories."

"Mom and dad – can't that wait until we're older?" Lilly

asked. "We're not into that whole dating stuff yet."

Ethan quickly interjected: "Good! You two are too young. Now, remember – no dating until…" Ethan trailed off, waiting for the girls to finish the sentence.

And they did. "Until dad says so." Both Violet and Lilly said the same thing in rhythm, just as if they'd been brainwashed from a young age by their father.

Their programmed response made Ethan smile and look at Rose. "Bet you didn't know I taught them that."

"Great, I'll let you handle them at that age, then. I'll worry about their younger years, and you handle them when they're teenagers. I'm happy to take that deal!"

Rose's quick comeback left Ethan laughing in the car's front passenger seat.

"We're here!" Rose soon said.

The girls didn't notice what their parents did next, otherwise it would have tipped them off to the real reason they were getting ice cream. After Rose parked the car, she picked up Eugene's car seat, which held him fast asleep cradled inside. Then, with her other arm, she went and held Ethan's hand, who was standing right next to his car door. Rose's collarbone still hurt somewhat despite having made progress healing over the past month. But she managed through the pain. Instead, she wanted to help Ethan in the more permanent adjustment in life that he was going through.

But their kids didn't see or hear their mother lead Ethan into the café, telling him where steps were located so that he wouldn't trip on them.

"You'd think I'd have this place memorized," Ethan said to Rose. "I mean – I've recalled our first date here several times. I remember it so vividly."

"What type of ice cream did I have then?" Rose tested her husband.

"Oh easy – cookie dough. What type did I have?"

"I wasn't staring at your ice cream." She bluntly said, one-upping Ethan. Rose was a killer for romantic comments, and that one should win an award.

"I remember how we couldn't stop holding hands almost right from the beginning," said Ethan.

"Looks like we still can't." Again, with Rose's award-winning response.

"Look at you," Ethan said, trying to flirt, "I spent all these years painting romantic-era paintings and you still out-do me with even more romantic lines."

"What can I say, your paintings had an effect on me."

Ethan squeezed his wife's hand to let her know both that he appreciated her compliment and that she again topped him with yet another romantic comment.

Rose continued: "So are you going to take the lead with the girls, or should I?"

"Well, let's start with the ice cream and then we'll go from there." Ethan was trying to avoid the topic of how to discuss his blindness with his daughters. He knew it was time to tell them. He just hadn't thought yet about the best way to handle it.

Ethan leaned down to his two daughters. "Anything you want." Their eyes both lit up. "I mean it – order whatever you want tonight. It's a special place for your mother and I."

Immediately, Lilly squinted her nose. "Ew, Dad – we said we don't wanna hear about that stuff."

The young girls definitely knew how to take their dad's offer for granted. The ice cream on their cones were piled so high that their eyes weren't even visible when the cone was held up to their mouths. Rose, Ethan, and their daughters just enjoyed a few minutes eating ice cream around a table before Rose decided it was time.

"Girls – there's something serious that your father and I need to talk to you about."

"I knew it," Violet interjected, "Mom's already pregnant again."

Ethan and Rose couldn't help but burst laughing out loud. After collecting herself, Rose kept explaining why they were really out at the café. "No, we're definitely not pregnant again." She then looked to her husband and squeezed his hand to signal that he should take over.

"Girls, your mom is right. We took you out for ice cream to butter you up." Ethan said lightheartedly.

Rose was thrilled to hear that Ethan was not being overly emotional about how he was handling it with the girls. She'd decided to let her husband break his news to them however he felt was necessary. The moment where he had told her was emotional enough. She was glad that they'd had that close, tender moment between them. But she knew it was time for Ethan to try and move on past the emotional baggage which his limitation weighed on him. So, Ethan's initial joking was a relief.

"Girls," Ethan continued. "I need to let you know that sometimes things don't always go the way you plan in life – and that's perfectly okay." Ethan hadn't planned what to say to them, so he was kinda surprised that he was phrasing things this way. It was almost as if he was really telling himself it was okay for the first time. He could sense that Violet was about to jump at guessing what he was talking about, so he kept talking to prevent her from detracting from the topic.

"Violet, do you remember how I looked kinda funny when I was painting you?" The girl nodded, not sure now of where this was going.

"Oh yeah," agreed Lilly, "I noticed that too."

"Well, girls, it's because I have vision issues – problems with my eyesight."

The girls sat there, no longer even licking their ice cream, unsure of what specifically their dad was trying to explain to them. After just a couple seconds of silence, Violet asked: "You mean, like – you need glasses?"

"No, girly, glasses won't help me." Ethan realized he needed to be a little bit more blunt. "I'm losing my eyesight. I'm going blind." Even though the words he spoke were direct, Ethan's tone was loving. It was as though he was being the strong example a parent needed to be during a hard time. But, really, inside was a storm – a hurricane of emotion swirling as he finally divulged to his entire family what he had kept secret for so long. But the look in his eye was one of love and understanding towards whatever reaction his children would have.

Ethan was then swept off guard by his eldest daughter's moving reaction. "It's okay, daddy. We still love you."

"Yeah, of course we do," Violet also chimed in.

Ethan couldn't help but choke up at the immeasurable love his young daughters expressed. "Oh, come here, you two." He said as he pulled them both in for a hug – one in each arm as he sat in between them at the table.

When he released them from his embrace, Violet asked a question that only her young bluntly-inquisitive mind could ask. "Does that mean I don't have to brush my hair anymore?"

"What?!" Ethan blurted out.

"Yeah – does this mean I don't have to bush my hair anymore since you won't be able to see what it looks like?"

"Why would you ask that?" Ethan inquired.

"Well, because every morning when I don't want to brush my hair, mommy says that I have to brush it so that I look good for you."

Ethan smirked across the table at his wife, who also couldn't hold in her laughing.

"Yes," Rose said jokingly. "And since daddy can't see us, we also don't have to try and stay skinny." The kids burst out laughing. "That's why I took you here. Now we can eat *as much* ice cream as we want!"

When the laughing from the family died down, Ethan interjected: "Now, hold on. I haven't gone totally blind yet. I can still see you from the side…" When he realized that his comment was taken a bit too seriously, he followed up: "… so you can't get chubby yet … which means you gotta give me some of your ice cream!" Ethan yelled out right as he lunged down and took a lick from Lilly's cone.

But Ethan froze immediately at what he heard next.

"Ethan?" A female voice from behind him asked.

Ethan had heard that a blind person's other senses become magnified to compensate for the vision loss. But he didn't realize the truth about that until at this very moment.

It was a distant voice – not from length, but from memory. One among many that he had locked out from the pain of his self-inflicted seclusion in life. It had been many, many years since he'd heard her voice, but his overcompensating sense of hearing quickly recalled the source of her voice. Even though it had probably been since he was a teenager – almost twenty years ago – since he heard her voice, he knew immediately who it belonged to.

His younger sister.

Chapter 17

At this moment, Ethan really wished he could see detail in the faces of his sister and, especially, his wife. He seldomly ever spoke about his family to Rose, who had never met them. And at the moment he heard his sister's voice, it quickly occurred to Ethan that he had never said a word to Rose before about any of his siblings. So, he just remained frozen by the shock of the unexpected voice from his past surprising him in this enjoyable evening out with his family. Though it was really just a few seconds that he remained frozen in place, it felt like an eternity.

"Ethan, is that really you?" She again asked.

Ethan turned around. As he did so, Rose switched chairs with Lilly so that she was now sitting next to her husband.

All of the emotions inside of Ethan conjured up by this unexpected voice swirled around inside of him like a depiction of The Starry Night painting. In just the instant that he had to react, he felt dread for not telling his wife about his siblings. He felt dread in not knowing what to say to a sibling he hadn't seen in forever. And he still felt desolate and left out of the family which never came to visit him even once in his studio.

He could have acted in dismissiveness toward his sister, but he didn't. Instead, he feigned a smile. Just as with the confrontation with his father-in-law a month ago in the hospital, Ethan felt as though he could hide behind the fact that he couldn't see his sister's face.

"Hey, Claire – how are you?" Ethan finally asked back in response. Rose knew her husband well enough to sense hurt in his voice. So, Rose squeezed his hand in support, even though Ethan didn't feel like he deserved any support from his wife – he never even told her about his siblings.

"How am I?" She asked rhetorically in excitement that she stumbled upon her long-lost brother. "I'm great! I can't believe it's really you, Ethan. After all these years…"

"You know…" Ethan was about to say something defensive to his sister about how she could have come to visit him at any time in his studio, but he didn't. He didn't have the chance to due to Rose cluing him in more on what he couldn't see.

"Claire, it's good to meet you. I'm Rose, his wife. Are these your two children?"

Ethan got Rose's hint immediately. Now was not the time

to place the blame on his family for not coming to see him.

"Oh yes, your kids," Ethan said directing his attention to the two shadows he saw on each side of his sister.

"Ethan, this is Naomi," Claire introduced. "And this is her brother, Russell."

Ethan reached out and shook Naomi's hand, hoping that his guess at her general location was close enough for him to extend his hand. While shaking her hand, he couldn't tell the ages of the two kids. So, he turned and smiled at Rose next to him, to get a glimpse of them both in his peripheral vision.

"Naomi – how old are you?" Ethan asked while still shaking his niece's hand.

"I'm four – we're twins!" Naomi exclaimed enthusiastically.

"Is that so?" Ethan asked, while then reaching out to shake his nephew's hand. "You both are so big – four is getting old, you know." Ethan found his nephew's name an obvious reference to his father as being the namesake. "And, Russell – you must be named after your grandfather, right?"

"You bet I am!" The boy said proudly.

"And how is he doing?" Ethan asked, intrigued by what the boy would say.

The last year had especially been difficult on Ethan from his adjustment to being blind. Even though Ethan had reason enough to focus on just himself and his family through his disability, something about his struggles during the last year often made his mind wonder toward how his family was doing – especially his father. Perhaps it was the now distinct feeling of impermanence from his vision loss, but Ethan had often considered reaching out to his father.

Ethan remembered the days where he would follow his father into the city and wait in his office until he could escape to Eugene's art gallery. Ethan recognized now that he had been just a young boy passionately interested in learning about the arts. But he still often dwelled on all the time he had passed up which he could have spent with his dad. Now having a son of his own, Ethan found himself easily able to put himself in his father's position. As a father, Ethan often thought about how he would react to his son falling in love with something other than his passion. Of course, Ethan knew that he would support his son in any way that he could to pursue what it was that he enjoyed. But that's where Ethan's deep-seeded regret with his father came in – he never even gave his father the chance to support him. Instead, Ethan lied to his father and deceived him about what he was doing each lunch hour. The same went with his mother, too – he never filled either of them in to what it was that he was passionate about.

It was this regret that led to an overshadowing fear to rekindle any relationship with his parents. He knew he owed them an apology. He just couldn't get the courage to repair a bridge that had broken so long ago. So, instead, he rationalized to himself that it was his parents who didn't want him in their life – because they had never come to visit him at his gallery. So, when Ethan asked his nephew about how his dad was doing, Ethan was genuine in learning anything he could about his father.

"Don't do that, Ethan." His sister said abruptly, ruining any chance for Ethan to learn about his father.

"Do what?"

"Please don't put my son in the middle of whatever it is you have against dad … against any of us."

Ethan was shocked. For the first time ever, he was learning about his family's perspective of his relationship to them. And he had no idea what his sister was talking about.

"What I have against you?" He asked, sincerely naïve about what Claire had just said. Rose squeezed his hand, signaling that this was probably not a good time or place to raise the issue – especially in front of their own kids. She may not know exactly what had gone on between Ethan and his family, but she knew one thing: he never told her about his siblings. So there was probably more to be said, and now was not the time.

Rose's squeeze reminded Ethan again to not go down that path, just as her earlier squeeze had done as well.

"Claire, I meant it. How is dad doing?"

"Can I sit for a moment, Ethan?" Claire asked, her tone instantly turning serious. "We should talk really quick before we get going."

Thrillingly, his girls instantly hit it off with Claire's kids and they started talking on the other end of the table while the adults sat on the other side. Rose had heard Lilly ask her newfound relatives what their favorite type of ice cream was, but Rose instead focused on the important conversation happening between her husband and Claire.

Ethan listened intently to whatever his sister needed to tell him. Whatever they thought about how he perceived them was totally wrong, but that was not as important as listening to what she had to say about his father.

"Ethan, I don't know how to put this, so I'm just going to be straightforward ... Ethan, what are you looking at?" Claire asked, noticing that Ethan was not looking directly at her. He had guessed where she had sat down at and tried to look her in the face, but was about a foot off to her right.

Claire saw this, and then looked down and noticed how Rose was holding his hand. It wasn't just a couple holding hands, it was firm and with purpose. Claire read the situation.

"Ethan, you're blind, aren't you?" Claire's voice cracked. Despite harboring years of hurt inside of her, thinking that her older brother didn't want anything to do with her, she felt hurt for him at this realization.

A tear fell from the corner of Ethan's eye – he could hear it in his sister's voice that she felt empathy for him. And he was deeply appreciative of this.

"Not totally ... yet ..." He trailed off, before a realization suddenly hit him. "How did you know?" He asked the question aloud, but already knew the answer. And his suspicion was confirmed by Claire's poignant words.

"Because dad is, too."

Ethan wasn't shocked. He was hurt – hurt for his father. He knew exactly what his dad had gone through. To his father, vision was just as necessary for his passion of neurosurgery as it was for Ethan's passion. They shared a common tragedy. But only, Ethan knew that his father's pain must have been far worse because his father was missing one thing that Ethan had: support from his family. And Ethan knew it was his own fault that his father didn't feel supported by his whole family.

Whereas Ethan was much more hurt by the news than shocked by it, Rose was dumbfounded. She had to ask the question that Ethan's sorrow and regret clouded: "Claire, is it hereditary?"

Claire shook her head. "I don't know. Until I saw Ethan, I had thought it was just dad. But now, well … I don't know … it might be."

With Rose holding Ethan's hand, Claire reached out and touched his other hand. "Ethan, I'm sorry, but that's not all I need to tell you."

Ethan fought to stay tough. He knew he had let his younger sister down all her life while growing up, but he was going to still try and show her strength through whatever other bad news she was going to say.

Ethan heard his younger sister's voice crack as she said it. "Ethan, dad is not doing well – he doesn't have long at all. You need to come see him – soon."

He could tell from the tone of her voice that his sister was scared. This must have been a recent development for her. He didn't know his sister, and felt exceedingly remorseful for how he had let her down all those years. Inside, Ethan wanted to crack. Not only was he remorseful about how he had treated his sister and other siblings, but he was even more remorseful toward how he had let his parents down. But he wouldn't let those inner fractures show. He wanted to try and be the rock that his sister needed, since he could tell that it was something she'd just found out too.

Ethan moved his hand out from under his sister's hand and reached up to touch her face. As he traced the outlines of her face, he painted the image of a woman who was in distress from the frailty of life.

Not all paintings he had created through the years were ones of young romantic couples swept away in the happiness of their romantic adventure. Indeed, few of them were. Romanticism wasn't just about the romantic love that can exist between two individuals. Rather, romanticism was a phrase used more generally for any work of art where the emphasis was on an individual's expression of emotion and imagination.

This is what Ethan felt in the contours of his sister's face. A great romantic work sat in front of him, one which demanded appreciation. For, her look conveyed a heightened sense of emotion and imagination at the sense of the looming loss of her beloved father. Though such emotions were undoubtedly sad and often unwanted, it was in those shadowy emotions that Ethan had always felt beauty. As, without the shadows, the light of the good times were not as appreciated.

Ethan's fingers finished tracing the outline of his sister's face by wiping a tear away from her eye with his thumb.

In a loving and understanding tone, Ethan calmed his sister. "It's okay, Claire. Everything will be okay."

Much more could have been said between the two siblings, but it didn't need to be. Claire could have been skeptical of her brother's statement – after all, he had been absent from their lives for so long – but she wasn't. She soaked up the strength and reassurance from her older brother like a sponge formed through years-worth of desire to know her brother.

She was about to say thank you to him, but Ethan's next words surprised him. "Claire, you feel like you look just like mom."

Ethan's comment sent a shiver down Claire's spine and put a smile on her face through the tears.

"And how is mom doing?" Ethan asked, now turning his attention to the woman which he knew he owed just as sincere of an apology to.

"She's strong. She's *so* strong, Ethan. She's the biggest blessing in the world to dad. Without her, he probably wouldn't have made it very long in his condition."

Ethan turned and looked at Rose, who sat there taking in the raw moment. Ethan knew exactly what kind of woman his mother was, because he was lucky to have just as strong and supportive of a woman in his life. And his simple reply exuded that knowledge. "I know."

Through Claire's tears, she cracked an invitation. "Come see for yourself. Please, Ethan. They miss you. We all do."

"We all? … who?"

"All of us, Ethan. All four of us siblings are in town – because we figured that dad didn't have much time…" Claire trailed off, her voice cracking again at the thought that she didn't have much time left with her father.

"Everyone will be there?"

"Yes, Ethan. We're all back home. Please come by –

tomorrow, please – he doesn't have much time."

"Claire?"

"Yes, Ethan."

"I'm so sorry that I wasn't there for you."

Ethan's sincere apology hung in the air due to Claire not having anticipated it. Ethan's voice trembled as he asked a question in follow up. "And Claire? Do you really think dad wants to see me?"

Ethan's question showed his vulnerability about how he truly felt that he'd let his parents down – how he really took blame for his fractured and distant relationship with his family through the years.

The tone in Claire's voice radiated truthfulness, sending tears streaming down Ethan's cheeks. "Absolutely."

Through the tears, Ethan managed: "Then we'll be there tomorrow."

Chapter 18

The car ride to his parents' house was strangely quiet –
even his children were quiet in the back seat. That never
happened.

But then Violet broke the silence. "Where are we going
again?"

"We're going to my parents' house – your grandparents'
house. You'll also see your cousins, aunts, and uncles."

"Yeah, remember?" Lilly told her sister. "We just saw
some of them last night."

"Oh, yeah! I liked them." She paused as a thought entered
her mind. Curiously, she asked that thought. "But, why haven't
we seen them before?"

Ethan glanced awkwardly to his wife, letting his shame at
not having them previously in their lives be easily observed on
his face. He wished that he could see his wife's reaction.

But Rose answered the children, being the angel that she
always managed to be. "Well, I'm just glad that we get to see
them now! I can't wait."

She turned and looked to her husband, who smiled back at her.

"You know," Rose said to him. "I'm just now starting to wonder if, after all these years, *you're* the one who really is a serial killer." Her tone was sarcastic, giving Ethan a hard time.

"Oh, c'mon Rose. Stop it. I'm not really in the mood right now to…" Ethan began before Rose continued to tease him.

"You see? That's exactly what a serial killer would do – dodge the inquiry." Ethan smirked, giving in to her playful banter to lighten the mood up. "No – really. I mean, all these years I joked with you about being one, but all along you hid your real identity from me. Your real past is a mystery. That's a pure serial killer thing to do if you ask me."

Ethan turned and looked out the window, recognizing her joke but also trying to move past it. But Rose wouldn't have anything to do with his solemn mood. She nudged him on the shoulder. "Oh, c'mon Ethan – I'm just joking."

"Mom?" Violet's inquisitive nature interrupted.

"Yes?"

"What's a serial killer?"

Rose and Ethan instantly laughed out loud. "You started it," Ethan said smiling. "So, you finish it."

Rose paused for a moment. She struggled between telling the truth, but also wanting to shield her young daughter from what a serial killer really was. If she told Violet what it really meant, it would keep her up for nights – there'd be no way that any of them would get any sleep for the next week due to the young child's unfettered imagination. So, Rose instantaneously decided it wasn't worth it and made up the first thing that came to her mind.

"It's someone who likes ... ice cream." She said, figuring it would blow over.

"Oh," Violet reacted and, luckily, she did not ask any more questions about it.

"Nice one," Ethan said.

"Thank you," Rose astutely responded, taking pride in her cleverness at making the situation blow over.

Rose then asked the question that had been on her mind since last night. "Ethan, why didn't you tell me about your family? You always blew the subject off, making it seem like they didn't want to be part of your life."

"They didn't want to be in it." He said defensively, though he still knew that there had somehow been a large miscommunication and misunderstanding between him and his family.

"Well, Claire certainly made it sound like that wasn't the case last night."

"Yeah, I just found out that last night. I'm still trying to understand that." Ethan wasn't mad at Rose. Rather, he was just flabbergasted by learning that his perspective of his family had somehow been wrong for all these years.

"What happened, Ethan?"

"I mean – I don't know where to begin."

"Ethan, we've got a while left until we get there. Start where it makes sense to you."

Ethan knew his wife. She was beautiful inside and out. Her patient willingness to listen to his issues, without being offended that he'd never told her in all the years before, was yet another of the countless ways that she showed her inner beauty. And Ethan was correct. Rose wanted him to vent to her prior to arriving at his parents' house. Venting there would lead to no good, so she knew it needed to come out before then.

Ethan's eyes faced forward, but his peripheral vision stared out the car window watching the trees pass by as he divulged years' worth of inner turmoil in just a few minutes.

"I'm the oldest of five kids – I have two sisters and two

brothers. It sounds like you'll meet them. Well, I'm about five years older than the next one. And so as I got older my parents always seemed to be preoccupied with them instead of me. Anyways, to jump ahead – the day I met you was the day I told them that I was moving out. And when I told them that night, I …"

"Night? You mean, you had told them at Eugene's memorial that night right before you met me?"

"Yeah – like the moment right before I saw you standing there…" Ethan drifted off, remembering that life-changing portrait of a scene in his mind. "… Anyways, that's not the point. I had told them that if they ever needed me, then I would be at the studio. But they never came. None of them did – my parents or my siblings. After a while I figured that they didn't need me in their lives so I just built a wall up. And that's really the brunt of it."

"That's so sad, daddy," Violet said from the back seat, revealing that the two girls had been listening the entire time.

But the sound of her voice mixed with the surprise that they'd been listening actually sent Ethan and Rose into laughter again.

"Well – it wasn't that sad. The whole time I had you."

Ethan cheered up. "Besides, we get to see them all now!"

As soon as he said that, Rose pulled into his parents' drive way.

"Wow, is that the house you grew up in?" Lilly asked, amazed by how large it was. While their family certainly lived in a sizeable house from the estate that Eugene had passed to Ethan, his parents' place still put it to shame.

"You ran away from *that*?" Rose agreed with Lilly, while giving her husband a hard time.

Her joking made Ethan smirk. As he opened the car door to get out, he remarked. "Oh, yeah – and my dad was a neurosurgeon." He said it in jest to explain the large estate in front of them.

"You didn't have to tell me that – I could have guessed it," Rose said in awe.

Through the joking, though, Rose could easily tell from holding her husband's hand that Ethan grew more nervous the closer they got to the front door. At the front door, she turned and looked at him. "Ethan, don't worry. You will do great. We're here for you."

Ethan's heart nearly leapt out of his chest as he reached to knock on the front door of his childhood home. He had no idea what to expect from anyone, and he knew that he deserved any disdain which may be expressed toward him. But, still, his hopes were so extremely high that his parents' love for him would somehow surpass his mistakes. Especially in this bleak hour of his father's life.

The door creaked open slowly.

"Ethan?" The faint voice of his mother asked in disbelief, as if seeing a son who she thought had died. "Ethan is that really you?"

Ethan couldn't see his mom directly, but he didn't need to. A tear fell slowly down his cheek answering his mom. "Yes, mom. It's me." He brushed aside his emotion, though, by introducing his family. "Mom, this is my wife, Rose. And these are our kids – your grandchildren – Lilly, Violet, and Eugene."

Ethan turned his head to the side to see from his peripheral vision his mother's look of shock as she held her cheeks in excitement and emotion.

"Oh, Ethan," she said before holding her arms out to embrace him. She pulled her son in close, and Ethan felt the frailty of her body in age as he pressed against her. "I've missed you *so* much. So much."

With his mother holding his head into her, Ethan could

no longer hold in his tears. "Mom, I'm so sorry."

"Oh, Ethan – you have nothing to apologize for." She let go of their embrace. "I'm just so happy you came back." She shifted her attention to his family so as to avoid getting more emotional. "And you have such a beautiful family! I'm Helen," she introduced herself to the rest of his family, "come on in."

Ethan imagined that a rush of memories would return to most people when returning to their childhood home for the first time. But it was different for him. The moment he stepped inside, a rush of regret instead filled him. Regret for not seeking out any of his family years earlier.

And now that regret was staring him in the face as he saw his two brothers, two sisters, and each of their families sitting in the living room waiting for his return. But none of them were scornful or expressed any criticism toward him as he hugged each one and introduced his family to them. Ethan felt as though he was living a dream – like he had drifted asleep on the car ride there and was dreaming about what he hoped would happen. Only, this was real. And as much as he felt that he didn't deserve any of it, the warmth of each moment embraced him in love.

But as much as he looked forward to seeing his siblings

again, there was really only one thought on his mind. His father. Where was he?

After reuniting with each of his siblings, Ethan turned to his mother. "Mom, where's dad?" His heart beat loudly in his chest, hoping that he wasn't too late – that death hadn't robbed him of the moment with his father since he learned about his rapidly decreasing health last night.

But his mom's words brought relief. "He's been sleeping in his bed. Should we go see if he's awake?"

Ethan took Rose's hand to help guide him down the hall toward his father's bedroom.

"No, Ethan," Rose said. "I'll let you have a moment alone with your father."

But Ethan gripped hard on her hand. "Rose, no – I'd like you to be there … in case this is the only chance you have to meet him." Ethan found it difficult to say those last words aloud, recognizing that this could also be his last time to see his father.

But before Ethan turned to walk down the hallway, he looked straight at his siblings and their families, who were entertaining his children. Ethan's question cut through the air as his pupils looked aimless into the room. "Are …" He cleared his throat, having a tough time recognizing out loud his weakness. "Are any of you like me and dad?" He couldn't even get the strength to say what he meant more specifically.

"You mean, blind?" One of his younger brothers asked.

Ethan just nodded.

That same brother responded calmly. "No, Ethan. It's just you and dad."

Ethan choked back tears at the good news. "Good. I'm really glad." He cleared his throat. "I, uh … I may not be able to see your families very well, but I can still tell that you each have beautiful families." He quickly turned away down the hall, trying to avoid the emotion of his regret and thankfulness for their acceptance.

Besides, for as difficult and emotional as it was to see his mother and siblings again, Ethan knew that was only the tip of the iceberg. Rose led him down the hall behind his mother. They stopped and his mother turned to them.

"I think I'll give you both a minute alone with him before I come to check-up on him, if that's okay." His mom said. She then kissed Ethan's cheek and returned down the hall to entertain her grandchildren.

Rose turned and looked her husband in the eye. "Ethan,

you have a beautiful family. They love you. Things will be alright, I know it."

But just at that moment, they heard Ethan's mom offer the grandkids ice cream.

"Alright!" Violet exclaimed with such excitement that it could easily be heard down the hall. "I want to be a serial killer!"

Rose and Ethan's jaws dropped in embarrassment, but also laughter at the irony of the situation.

"I better go explain things, Ethan. I'll be in with you two in a few minutes." Rose then kissed Ethan on the cheek and whispered "good luck" in his ear before darting down the hallway to fix the situation.

Ethan stared at the door to his father's room, anxious to see his father for the first time in many years. There was so much that he wanted to say, but knew there was so little time. Ethan's heartbeat was audible as he turned the handle to open the door.

"Dad?"

Chapter 19

"Helen, is that you?" The frail, voice of Ethan's father asked.

"No, dad – it's me. Ethan."

His dad paused for what was probably only a second but felt like hours to Ethan, unsure of how his father would react.

"Is it you? Is it really you?" He asked. His father's voice was weak and barely much more than a whisper, but the sound of hope in it was still enough to ignite Ethan's emotions afire. His dad wanted him. His dad missed him. Ethan could easily tell this from the hope in his father's voice.

Ethan scuffled over to his father's bedside, having difficulty in the dark and without his vision. But he found a chair nestled next to his bed which others had obviously been using before him.

His father, Russell, extended his right arm out to search for Ethan next to him. Despite his poor eyesight, Ethan was able to see the feebleness of his father's arm as it extended aimlessly outward for him.

"Come here, my boy." Russell asked, with the wisp of air consuming as much of his voice as the words he spoke.

Ethan lowered his face down to his father's bedside. Russell's weak fingers held his face in his hand. His fingers traced his son's face, trying to create an image in his mind of the man that his young boy grew up to be. Ethan couldn't hold in the tears as his father was now doing exactly what he had taught Violet to do the night he finished his portrait of her.

"Dad, I've lost my vision too."

Russell paused tracing his face for a moment, being caught off guard by his son's mournful statement. Ethan was sure that if he traced the outline of his father's face that he would feel a reciprocal well of tears. His father's deep hurt from the bad news was heard in his voice.

"I'm *so* sorry, my boy."

"Dad?"

"Yes, son?"

"Dad - I'm scared."

Ethan's voice trembled. Never before had Ethan admitted this to anyone. Being in front of someone who could understand his feelings allowed him to admit it for the first time. It was the purpose for which he hid his blindness for so long, instead choosing the mistake of lying to his family. But to know that he could confide his fear in his father was more of a relief than he could have ever imagined.

His entire life, he felt different than his father – like they had absolutely nothing in common. He went a different path and chose to not return, choosing in ignorance his route to art over the route to science that he had always thought his father desired for him to follow. But now, their paths converged. And in that convergence – in the shadows of the dark room, and in the shadows of their vision loss – there was beauty. And that beauty was captivated by his father's next words.

"Ethan?"

"Yes, dad."

"I love you, son."

His father's words of redemption sent tears flooding into Ethan's eyes. But before Ethan could compose himself to say a word back, his father continued: "Tell me about your art."

His father's words caught him by surprise, leaving him even more tearful - one of the first things his father asked about was what Ethan had always thought his father never cared about. He didn't know if his dad was asking it as a way to answer his fears, or because his father regretted never really paying attention to it.

"But you saw some of it that night in the gallery – the night I saw you last."

"No, son – I didn't."

Ethan's heart dropped. He knew the answer to this next question, but asked it anyways. "Why not? You were standing right by it."

"Ethan, I was almost blind then."

Ethan could no longer conceal his deep sympathy for his father and the endless amount of pain he must have brought his parents due to his narrow-sighted selfishness. The tears streamed down his face, yet Ethan managed to smear them away through his words.

"Well, I'll tell you about my most prized painting. It's called The Rose, and I drew it the night that I met my wife." Ethan didn't have the courage to explain that it was drawn that same evening when he'd last seen his parents – and that didn't matter. Instead, Ethan described the painting in such detail to his father over the next several moments that he could tell that his father was picturing it in his mind.

"I see it," his father said while staring up at the ceiling. "I can see it so clearly, as if I was standing in front of it." He then patted Ethan's cheek with his hand. "Thank you, my boy, for that. I needed to see something beautiful."

Ethan wanted to pour out his heart to express his deep regret to his father, but he didn't have a chance as his father spoke again.

"Hold onto that and you will never give into your fear."

"Hold onto what?"

"Rose."

The poignancy of his father's answer hung in the air, striking Ethan with his directness. He wasn't talking about the painting, he was talking about his wife. And Ethan knew it.

"Dad, I'm so sorry. All these years … I shouldn't have …"

"Sorry for what?" His father asked weakly.

Though the laundry list was long, Ethan said the first things that came to his mind. "I'm sorry I didn't follow in your footsteps to be a doctor. I'm sorry I lied to you about what I did every lunch when I'd come to the city with you. I'm sorry …." But Ethan didn't have a chance to continue, as his father cut him off sternly.

"No. Don't be sorry – for *anything*." He said emphatically before coughing into a napkin that he held in his other hand.

When he put the napkin down, the bright hues of red on the napkin stood out to Ethan even through his blindness. They were that obvious - like red paint on a blank white canvas. Only this wasn't paint, it was blood - telling Ethan that his father's time was nearing an end. Ethan heard the bedroom door creak open behind him, and the voices which followed signaled who was entering.

"It's just us, Ethan. It's Rose and your mom."

Both of the women entered the room and Helen turned on a dim light for them before they came and sat near Ethan.

Undeterred from utilizing this opportunity – which might be his last – to apologize to his father, Ethan continued: "But I am, dad. I should have been a better son. I should have been in your life – in mom's life too…" Ethan trailed off, glancing over to where he saw the outline of his mom sitting across the bed from him.

His father went to speak again, but coughed hard into his napkin instead. Unable to get out words, he pointed with his other hand to the desk sitting just behind Ethan and Rose.

"Go ahead," his mother said, also pointing to the desk. "They're in the top draw - I think you should know …"

"Know what, mom?" Ethan asked.

Rose got up and opened the top desk drawer, finding a large wad of envelops. She sat next to Ethan and opened the first envelope on top, reading the handwritten letter contained within it aloud for her husband to hear.

"Dr. Mr. & Mrs. Cooley,

I met your son today. I write this letter to you because I wanted to let you know that I offered him an apprenticeship in my art gallery, and I didn't want to do so without informing his parents.

Your son is extremely talented – more so than any student I have taught in all my years heading the Buckhorn Art Company. He doesn't just see art – he feels it, as though it's a sixth sense for him. I would be deeply honored to teach your son what I know, for I believe painting will have a large role in his future.

Sincerely,
Eugene Turner"

Rose was dumbfounded when she finished the letter. Even though she didn't have a clear picture of the relationship between Ethan and his parents, Rose knew the significance of this letter. And that significance hit heavily on Ethan.

Ethan's jaw fell agape the moment he heard Rose read the

first sentence. He was stunned.

"You both knew – the whole time." Ethan said through his shock.

His father moved his hand over to Ethan's hand on the bedside, patting it to signal that they knew. His mother nodded: "Yes, Ethan. Of course we knew. Read the next one, Rose, please."

Rose opened the next envelope, which was addressed from his parents to Eugene.

"Eugene,

Already we feel indebted to you for your kindness and willingness to help our son. We must admit that we have long felt lost with him. He hides his easel and paints from us, somehow believing that we don't know or care about his passion. Perhaps that drives him – we truly don't know. And the thing is, we are scared in thinking that we may never understand what drives his artistic inspiration.

Our love for our son is unending, and for that reason we are thrilled to accept your gracious offer for his apprenticeship. Please keep us updated on not only our son's wellbeing but also his creations.

Gratefully,
Russell & Helen Cooley."

"Son," his mother said immediately as his father continued to hold his hand on the bed, "of course we always knew and cared about you. From the moment you could pick up a pencil, you were gifted with something that we didn't understand. You just always needed your independence from us to express it – and that was something which even Eugene recognized and supported through the years."

"We're proud of you, son." His father said faintly before coughing up more blood.

"Dad, I'm sorry," Ethan stuttered through his tears, shocked and overjoyed by what had just been revealed to him. All those years, his parents knew. Through his tears, Ethan recognized that his parents' love was showed for him much differently than it had been for his siblings. They showed their love for him by setting him free.

Ethan knew it and felt immeasurably appreciative and indebted to his parents for the love that they had actually been showing to him all those years. But at this late minute in his father's life, he had nothing tangible left to offer his father to say thank you.

However, he knew what his father would want most.

Ethan leaned over to his father, lying weakly on the bed

staring up at the ceiling. He put his lips next to his father's ear and simply whispered: "I love you, dad. I always have, and I always will."

Ethan was close enough to see a tear slowly fall down his father's cheek from his words, and Ethan could tell that unlike his prior tears from that evening – it was a tear of happiness. But that would be his father's last tear ever, as Ethan heard his father's breathing end while being perched next to his face.

Ethan knew his father just passed away. In the quite of the moment, Ethan lifted his hand and began to trace the outline of his father's face with his fingers, creating a portrait of his father in his mind. Nothing else in the room seemed to exist in this intimate, still moment between father and son, as Ethan grasped for something to remember the image of his father by.

After a moment, he finished and got up to hug his mother. "I'm so sorry, mom." He said humbly in her arms, obviously referring to her husband having just passed away.

"It's okay, Ethan. We've all said our goodbyes countless times by now."

His mother's words were recognition not only of her strength, but how his father seemed to hang on just long enough to want a final goodbye with his lost son. It felt so good to Ethan to embrace his mother in his arms after all these years, now understanding the boundaries of her love for him in giving him the space that was needed to develop his passion.

Many other words were said among the entire family that night, but as it was for Ethan with his art – it was the feelings which he experienced among his mother, siblings, and their families that mattered most. And it were those feelings which he knew he'd have to hold onto firmly in the coming days as he could feel that the last of his eyesight was quickly dissipating.

The car ride back from his parents' house was initially just as quiet as the car ride to his parents' house had been. But instead of being quiet due to the nervousness of going somewhere new to them, it was silent due to the feeling of warmth and joy that came from being welcomed back into his family.

Rose broke the silence by saying something that she'd been thinking of since the moment that she saw Ethan trace his deceased father's face on the bed. "Ethan, I think you should paint him – so you don't forget."

Ethan shook his head sideways, instantly knowing that he disagreed. "No, Rose. I don't have time."

"Well, I think you should try."

"No."

"Why not?"

"Because I'd rather paint you."

Chapter 20

"Are you ready to head out?" Ethan asked Rose as he put on his coat. He'd heard Rose line up a babysitter for the evening, so he was looking forward to being able to finally paint her portrait this evening. He was impressed that she was able to find a babysitter so quickly after he'd told her last night on their way from his parents' house that he needed to paint her.

"Whoa there. Wrong jacket," Rose said with a smile on her face. She retreated into their closet and pulled out the tuxedo suit that the owner of a distinguished art gallery always had to keep for special occasions. "You'll need this for tonight."

Ethan knew that this was one of those moments when he would see a sparkle in his wife's eye, but that was now beyond his abilities. Instead, he heard the excitement ring out from Rose's voice as she teased him about something which was being intentionally kept from him.

But still, Ethan was going to try and get it out of her – whatever she was withholding. "A tuxedo, huh? You know it's me that's supposed to paint you – not you painting a portrait of me … in a tuxedo!"

"Nice try, buddy," She said from the other room as she continued to get dressed for some mystery occasion. She'd obviously caught onto Ethan's attempt to find out what was really going on that evening. "Now, put it on."

Ethan tried to focus while putting on his tuxedo. He fumbled with his bowtie – but it wasn't because of his vision difficulties. Something else had drawn his attention from his periphery.

He saw his wife squirm and squeeze into her dress, carefully burning the outline of her figure into his brain – in case this was the last time he'd be able to study it. But it wasn't just her figure that had him distracted. She was putting on that black, polka dot dress with the rose-shaped broach which she'd worn on their date so many years ago. For as beautiful as she was back then, Ethan knew that her stunning beauty had only magnified with time. As he stood there silently watching her like a school boy who stumbled upon a lucky situation, he couldn't help but be swept away by her beauty. He knew he was that lucky boy who stumbled upon her in his galley so many years ago.

He watched her from the other room as she struggled to zip up her own dress, with her back turned toward him. Ethan walked over to zip up her dress slowly for her, making her jump in surprise when he first touched the zipper. After he zipped it up, he wrapped his arms around her from the back and cradled her in his arms. He slowly kissed her neck, feeling the sensual warmth and softness of her skin.

"Are you sure you're blind?" Rose asked in a flirtatiously mocking tone. "If you were blind, you wouldn't have been able to see me dressing…"

"It was all a ploy," Ethan retorted, "to let you think I couldn't see you."

Rose chuckled before turning around in his arms and kissing him on the lips. When she pulled away, she told him: "Okay, listen. I had something planned for you. And I want to warn you in advance, that I invited your family last night."

"Good!" Ethan was thrilled to hear that his family would now somehow be more present in his life, though he didn't know exactly what he was agreeing to.

"But listen, Ethan." Rose got serious. "I mean this. Tonight's a night to enjoy – no more tears. There's been enough tears lately. I planned this for you to enjoy."

"Okay," Ethan agreed. Again, he didn't know what he was getting himself into, so he didn't plan on shedding any tears.

"I mean that," Rose said sternly but with a glimmer of mocking in her voice. "You artists have such strong emotions – happiness, sadness, all of them. I know you experience the full palette of emotions," She said lovingly while straightening his crooked bowtie. "But tonight, there's no being sad. Just enjoy the moment."

Ethan nodded emphatically in agreement at her instruction. "Got it. I'll hide my emotions … like a redhead." That last phrase came out as a joke toward his red-headed wife, and he was lucky that she interpreted it as the joke that it was.

She pecked him on the cheek. "Very funny." She said before they turned to leave.

Ethan had no idea what to expect. And he definitely had no idea what was going on as he noticed that they were pulling up to park next to his own gallery. Habitually, he went to enter the studio's rear entrance, but Rose stopped him.

"Not tonight," she took his hand to guide him, "tonight, you use the front entrance."

The walk to the front was dark, leaving Ethan unable to

see in any detail all of the cars that lined the street and downtown Atlanta in front of the great Buckhorn Art Company.

Rose let go of her husband for a moment to open gallery's front glass door. Ethan could tell that the light was on already. But immediately as soon as the door opened, he knew what was going on – what Rose had planned.

An uproar of applause filled the halls of his gallery as he entered. He froze immediately and just looked around, taking in the sheer number of people who had come to greet him. The welcoming and congratulatory applause did not immediately die down; rather, it continued to grow for what felt like minutes on end – leaving Ethan with a deep, unequivocal feeling of accomplishment and appreciation. Even Rose let go of his hand and stood next to him, applauding the magnificence of his career and what he had turned the gallery into.

Rose had planned a retirement party for him. The retirement was forced on him by his vision loss, no doubt. But that certainly did not undermine his significant artistic achievements for himself, his vast amounts of students through the years, and the contribution of his gallery to the culture of downtown Atlanta.

The continued applause greatly overwhelmed Ethan. But he had promised Rose not to shed a tear this evening. So, he decided he could no longer take the constant applause without breaking his promise. He raised his hand in the air, both to reciprocate their acknowledgement and to also silence the crowd.

"I would say thank you – but I can't see who you are," Ethan said with a joking tone. Having come to terms with his vision loss during his conversation with his father the evening prior, he was now able to make a joke about it without feeling emotional. And it worked, the audience chuckled.

"But really, thank you to everyone for coming. I hope to say hi to many of you – but if I don't get to it, please do what both myself and my mentor Eugene Turner would want most: appreciate the art. It can convey so much more than my meager words can. Enjoy the evening!"

Ethan sought to wave the visitors off into an evening of enjoyment, but Rose quickly interjected. "Oh no you don't! Not yet!" She said. Rose had grabbed a couple of glasses of a drink on a platter next to her. She handed one to Ethan and raised the other in the air to make a toast to everyone staring at her in the halls of the gallery.

"Like many of you, I met Ethan in this gallery – actually, on a night very similar to this one where a great artist was being recognized. I was standing just down there," she pointed toward the hall where Ethan's painting 'Embrace the Light' still hung in the exact same spot.

She continued: "It was love at first sight for me, really." The audience reacted with "oohs" and "ahhs," but Rose's trademark whit quickly stepped in. "Oh, not love at first sight toward Ethan," she said smirking. "I fell in love with his art at the first sight of it."

The audience chuckled at her sly remark. But then Rose's tone turned serious. "And that's what he does – that's what great artists do. They move you. They provoke you. They inspire you. They don't just inspire you to find greatness in art, but they inspire you to want to express greatness in your own life – however that may be. And that's what Ethan Cooley has done for so many of us who gather this evening to celebrate the great influence he has had on each of us. So, to that, I say cheers!"

The halls echoed with the boisterous reciprocation of "cheers" and then everyone immediately started to turn and talk to neighbors. Ethan turned to convey his genuine gratitude toward Rose for her words, but she cut him off with a suggestion.

"Just listen, Ethan." She said in a voice just louder than a whisper in his ear. "Do you hear it?"

Ethan stood and listened. His eyes no longer allowed him to visualize the scene, so his ears instead overcompensated to do so. He heard the walls of the gallery withholding a wide range of conversation from a diverse group of people.

Some of their voices he recognized as prior students. Some of them were familiar voices from the general public who he'd gotten to know over the years as they would visit the gallery. Others were voices of customers – those who had purchased his paintings as commissions for either their own galleries or private residences from all over the country. He even heard the voice of Claire and some of his other siblings. Other voices he didn't recognize at all, telling him that strangers or members of the public had taken time out of their lives to come visit for the evening, despite not having a personal relationship to him. Regardless of who the individual was, Ethan was flattered.

"Yes, I hear them." He responded to his wife in awe of how his hearing was overcompensating for his vision loss.

Rose still whispered in his ear. "Can you see them now?"

"Yes."

"They're here for you and what you've accomplished, Ethan. Enjoy the evening."

Just then, a familiar voice approached him. "Ethan!" A female voice exclaimed.

"Bridgette!" Ethan was excited to hear a voice that he easily recognized.

"Ethan, I just wanted to say thank you again for helping me with everything. Teaching me how to paint and helping me kick start my studio." Bridgette was keen to only broadly reference Ethan donating his impressionist painting The Rose to her gallery, since she still was unsure of whether Rose had found out that he was the actual creator of it.

"You did it all yourself," he replied. "So, how have you been?"

"Oh, it's been great! I mean, it's nothing like what you have here, but I've been overwhelmed with the response. Anyways, I just wanted to take a moment of your time to say thank you again."

"It's been my pleasure, Bridgette. I'm sure I'll be dropping into your place again."

"Anytime," Bridgette said before disappearing into the crowd.

Next a man about ten years older than Ethan came forward toward Ethan and Rose. Rose helped Ethan out by explaining who was in front of them.

"Ethan, this is Robert Johansson – from New York, I believe. Is that right?"

"Yes, you have an excellent memory, Rose," complimented Robert.

"And you may remember that he commissioned one of your pieces" Rose's memory of Robert signaled just how much she had been involved with the business and sales aspects of the business for so many years. And that role would now become increasingly important in the coming years.

"Oh yes," recalled Ethan. "The commission was for a fantastic painting I entitled simply 'One Day.' I really enjoyed that one." Ethan reached out aimlessly to shake Robert's hand.

Robert helped guide Ethan's hand to his and the two men shook. "I just wanted to say thank you again. It's been a very popular piece up in New York, and you have a unique talent."

"Why, that's very kind of you," responded Ethan while smiling. The fact that this man had come all the way down to

Atlanta from New York meant a lot to Ethan. "I hope one day to make it up to New York to drop in."

"You're always welcome," replied the man. But another familiar voice then moved in to take Ethan's attention.

Ethan recognized that voice – it was a voice he actually was hoping not to hear tonight. His father-in-law, Earl. "Ethan, I have something I want to say."

Ethan stopped and listened hard, knowing there was a chance that he would have to take the high road with Earl despite the evening being to celebrate him.

"I'm sorry. I was wrong."

In everything Ethan thought might come out of Earl's mouth just now, an apology was nowhere in the universe of what he thought Earl would say. Ethan turned his head to the side to look in his peripheral vision to see if either Rose or her mom were prodding Earl's apology. But, strangely, they weren't.

And that apology continued. "I was wrong about you – about … well, everything. You have a very nice place here, and I'm sorry about your vision loss."

Ethan wanted to tear up, but again he'd promised Rose he wouldn't. That was how overjoyed he was at Earl's genuine apology. Ethan knew he could easily find a way to jab back at Earl by saying something like "I told you," or "I know you were wrong," but that wasn't Ethan's style. He'd painted so many different people into his art over the years that he'd recognized magnificence in people when it occurred. And this long overdue, redemptive and honest apology was the essence of such a magnificent trait in a person. This actually left Ethan admiring his father-in-law, just as he admired those qualities in his paintings.

"Thank you. But a lot of this is due to Rose, and you raised her. You made her the amazing woman she is. So, I owe you a large thank you." Ethan patted his father-in-law on the shoulder, which was essentially their man-equivalent of a hug. "Thanks for coming, I really mean that. And I hope you enjoy the evening – stay as long as you'd like."

"Thank you," Earl's voice cracked in humility before an excitable voice intervened.

"Wow, big brother, you have such a magnificent place!" It was Claire. "The only art I get to see all day are the scribbles of children."

"Well, some of the more modern-abstract paintings aren't much different," Ethan quipped. "And that's why I don't hang them in here."

Claire laughed. "Which one of yours is your favorite?"

"Oh, it's not in here," Ethan said without thinking. He was, of course, referring to his painting The Rose, but let his response slip. He quickly tried to cover for what he said because Rose still did not know that he was its painter. "…because I haven't painted it yet. I think my last painting before I lose my eyesight will be Rose's portrait. Hopefully I'll do that one soon."

It worked. Rose didn't suspect that he was really talking about a painting she was unaware of.

"Is there one in here I could go see before I have to leave to get the babysitter back home?"

"Oh definitely," Ethan said excitedly, "it's called 'Embrace the Light,' and it's hanging just around the corner over there." Rose squeezed Ethan's hand, signaling that she knew why it was his favorite.

Just then, Ethan's other siblings and his mother walked up.

"Ethan, this is the rest of your family."

After hugging them briefly, Ethan smiled while talking to them. "Thanks so much for coming. Mom – how are you doing?" He asked, referring to his father having passed away just the evening before.

"We had a busy day today making funeral plans for next week. Will you be able to come?"

"Of course," Ethan jumped. "I wouldn't miss it for anything. But how are you doing? … How are all of you doing?"

"Well," one of his brothers said, "we knew it would happen one day … one day soon, actually. It's surreal that he's gone, but we each kinda said our goodbyes a while ago."

Another of his sisters spoke, and the rest of his family nodded in agreement: "He's in a better place now, and that brings us peace."

His mother spoke again. "You know, there's something your father used to always say once he lost his vision that you might appreciate." Ethan could hear the effort in her voice to hold back her emotions, but he'd told himself that he wouldn't be caught up in the emotion. He had promised Rose to be strong, and he had done such a great job of it so far this evening.

"What's that, mom?"

"That Beethoven composed his greatest works after he

lost his hearing."

The thought rung true in Ethan, especially knowing it was what his father would hang his hopes on. But, for now, Ethan decided to focus on different advice from his father – to get through the tough times by holding onto hope.

"Thanks, mom. Maybe one day I'll get back into it. But I think I'll spend some time just focusing on what matters most to me." He looked at his wife and smiled.

"Ethan, I'm sorry that I never came to visit your gallery bef…" But before his mom could finish the sentence, Ethan cut her off.

"No, no. Not tonight. No tears and no apologies. There's been enough of that lately, and probably more to come." Ethan was referring to his wife's keen observation from earlier in the night. "Tonight, just enjoy yourself. Go explore the art, talk to new people, and enjoy the food!"

He hugged them again before they turned to go get lost in the night full of enjoyment.

And Ethan did the same. He met several knew admirers of his art, and also reminisced and laughed with numerous prior students. The night was full of memories and hope-filled wishes for the future of his gallery that genuinely left him looking toward the next chapter in his life.

But just as Ethan grew tired of accepting countless compliments from well-intentioned guests, the night slowly came to a close. The dim lights of the gallery's hallways left shadows in Ethan's bleak vision. But there was one shadow that he had grown extremely familiar with.

He saw the outline of his wife's figure perched in front of one of the classical paintings just a few feet down the hall from where the last of his guests had departed.

"What do you see?" Ethan asked that same question he had asked Rose the night he had met her while she unknowingly studied his own painting.

"I see a kiss," she said smirking, playfully referring to the painting The Kiss that Eugene had introduced Ethan to as a boy so long ago. But it was the playful way she said it that left Ethan intrigued by if there was another meaning to her answer.

As he got even closer, she held her hand out to him and drew him. Slowly, her lips touched his. Her kiss surprised him, as he had assumed that she was referring to the name of the painting. So, he didn't immediately react when he felt the soft sensual feeling of her lips caress his. His sensation of sight was nearly gone, but his other sensations were afire. He grabbed the back of her head as he drew her in, quickly escalating the intensity of their passionate kiss.

The two lovers stood alone under the dim lights of the deserted remnants of the upscale art gallery which just moments ago had been filled with celebration. Now, they were alone – but not just alone, they were together. Ethan knew that he was never truly alone as long as he had Rose. And Rose was embraced not just by Ethan's arms, but had always felt that she was truly embraced and appreciated by the man's endless appreciation for beauty. And to know that his capacity for appreciation had somehow found her from within the entire world made her feel like the most appreciated, desired person in existence.

It was that realization which made Rose pull away from their passionate embrace. "Everyone's gone," she said softly. "Will you paint my portrait now? I don't want you to forget what I look like."

"I was hoping you'd ask that tonight."

Chapter 21

The ambience of his art studio radiated. It was electric, as the intensity of his connection to Rose reinvigorated his desire to paint, despite his vision deficit. Ethan knew that, for the foreseeable future, this would be the last of his creations. Although it couldn't be his best painting, he was nonetheless going to try and capture her essence as perfectly as he could.

"Where do you want me to be?" She asked, leaving the specifics of the scene up to him.

"I need you to be close so I can try to make you out."

Rose moved a tall stool over to where his easel stood in front of where he'd began getting his paints ready. But instead of sitting on it, she took another two steps over and whispered in his ear. "Did you just say you need to make out with me?"

Just the sound of her taunting, enticing whisper sent a tingling sensation down his spine. He turned and faced her – his lips now perched right in front of hers. Rose expected her husband to push for needing to paint, and to thus push her back to get into positioning for the portrait. But he didn't. And that left her pleasantly, seductively enthralled. Instead, he slowly moved his lips an inch closer to hers, leaving the weight of his breath pulsing on her lips. Just the feeling of his breath sent a euphoric compulsion through her, desiring for him to draw his lips just the final inch closer to hers.

"I mean, is that what you want?" He taunted passionately.

She wanted to jump on him - to finish their celebratory night away without the children. But she didn't. Through the exhilaration of Ethan's unexpected response, she somehow found the instinct to try and think clearly. She knew that her short-term passions needed to be sacrificed for what was in Ethan's best long-term interest. He needed something to allow him to remember her face. Now was not the time to give into the temptation for anything other than having him paint her portrait.

Rose's only response was a chuckle as she backed away from him. Creating some distance between them was necessary if they were to shift focus toward the portrait. But still, it wasn't easy for Rose.

"Are you sure you're not totally blind yet? You can still see me?" She asked backing away from him and straddling the stool, returning her husband's taunting with her own visual teasing.

"You're killing me, babe. That dress ... your figure ..."

A sly smile adorned Rose as she knew that her taunting had won out. The frozen look on Ethan's face as he stared to the side to see her in his periphery signaled that he was beyond distracted from her flirtatiousness.

And what he said next signaled that he was not as willing to sacrifice the evening for his long-term good. "I mean – we can try painting again another night."

"Nope," Rose snapped. Her remark brought him back to earth, as she knew that she had to snap him out of his trance. "We can get a babysitter anytime, Honey. Now, paint." She then sat properly on the stool, forcing his focus to shift to the task at hand.

"Okay," if you say so. Though he tried hard to fix his attention on beginning the portrait, his desire to flirt with his wife had not yet ended. "I mean, normally I paint just from the shoulder up. But – babe – you ... in that dress ..." he trailed off, his imagination running wild. "I think I want to paint a portrait of all of you."

"Ethan ..." Rose was now working harder to have him focus on what needed to get done.

"Okay, fine," he gave up as he began sketching the outline of her face. "I find it suspicious, though, that you're the one who's so desperate to have the painting done. What are you gonna do – kill me and sell it for a fortune as my last great work?"

Rose smirked. "Oh, so it'll be worth a lot then, huh?" She joked while playing along with his scenario.

"You have no idea. It'll be worth the most of all of my works – except one, that is."

This last remark threw Rose for a loop. "Oh, really, which one?"

Ethan was of course referring to The Rose. He didn't plan to finally divulge to Rose right now, though, that he was the actual artist behind the painting which had hung in their study for years. But joking about it was his way of finally hinting that she didn't know all of his works. And on top of that, it was just plain fun messing with her.

"Oh, I can't tell you that. If I did, you'd definitely kill me and steal it. I still don't trust you at all – a woman as attractive as you only gets close to a blind guy like me because she wants something from him. You've definitely got to be a serial killer."

Rose appreciated her husband's persistent joking and

flirting, but she got serious for a moment. "Ethan, are you serious?"

"Yeah, I think you could be a serial killer … I mean, I've met your dad." Oops. Ethan didn't mean to say that last part, and he wasn't sure he even meant it after Earl's sincere apology earlier in the evening. But his joking accidently may have gone too far as he let it slip. He figured he was in trouble now.

"Ethan, I'm being serious."

"Wait, so I'm not in trouble for that last joke?"

Rose raised an eyebrow and smirked at her husband. "We'll talk about that later – but really, babe. What painting are you talking about?"

Ethan wasn't sure if he was lucky or not that Rose was skipping over a joke which on any other normal moment would have gotten him in the doghouse. Though he didn't want to be in trouble with her for it, he also did not want to talk any further about his most treasured creation.

"Oh, I was just joking."

Rose eyed him suspiciously. She couldn't tell whether or not he was hiding something. But she decided to let is pass for now.

Ethan tried to change the subject. "You now, for

someone so insistent on wanting your portrait painted, you sure are talking a lot. If your portrait turns out poorly, I'm just gonna blame it on you."

Rose took him up on his suggestion. She quietly sat on the stool, studying her husband. He had just mentioned having another painting that she didn't know about before quickly dismissing it. She didn't know if he had let something slip, or if he was joking as he had said. And she'd noticed him say something similar to Claire earlier in the evening as well – making Rose suspect that Ethan was now trying to conceal something. So, she studied him. But as she watched his movements, her inner dialogue quickly changed.

What began as skepticism in seeing if he was lying to her soon turned into observing his subtle actions. Every minutia of effort he made toward the canvas was devoured by her attention. She had often seen him paint many times before, but this was really the first time where she had *studied* him – just as he was studying her now. The way he held his brush between two fingers. The way he carefully swirled or dotted paints depending on the hues he sought to achieve. The way he squinted as he focused on detail. And with his vision loss, his focus was even more astute. Rose saw this in her husband, and fell in love with him all over again while studying him.

This was the man she was so lucky to have met all of those years ago. There was greatness not only in his work, but greatness radiating through all that he did in life. That greatness existed regardless of whether or not anyone was there to appreciate it – it was innate in the contours of his being. His passion for life, and his desire to emulate the beauty which he saw all around him shone from his soul for anyone who was lucky enough to have met this great man. And, in this silent moment between them, Rose knew she was that lucky person. Even though she knew that Ethan felt that *he* was the lucky one in their relationship, the fact he felt that way only made her crave stronger to be with him forever. Despite any vision loss or other issue that could come up between them in their life, this feeling which Rose now was experiencing was even more magnetic.

What felt like minutes to Rose as she drifted off in thought while posing for the portrait was really an hour. Ethan ended that hour by declaring his work as finished.

In eager anticipation for seeing the greatness of the completed work, Rose nearly jumped off of the stool and over to her husband's side. But when she turned to look at the painting, her heart dropped.

What had been deep feelings of appreciation toward Ethan quickly changed into feelings of sympathy and hurt for him as she saw what was on the canvas.

"Well? What do you think?" Ethan asked naively.

Staring at the painting made Rose quickly realize just how bad his vision loss was. She had always assumed that there was enough sight for him to be able to compensate and make out – with effort – detail in his surroundings. But now, she knew his eyesight was essentially gone.

On the canvas was a disjointed representation of a person. The outline of the face did not even connect, and the eyes were without shape. The entirety of her face looked as though it was a scrambled, random assimilation of parts nowhere near representing her – let alone any other specific person.

It was in this tough moment of realization that she knew she needed to be strong for her husband. A tear of empathy for her husband fell slowly down her cheek. She knew that his passion was now fully taken away.

"Speechless, huh? You said it would be my greatest work after all…" Ethan remarked. But the nervousness was heard in his voice. His attempt to fish for a compliment was the search for hope that he hadn't yet lost his ability to paint. But the nervousness heard in his voice gave away that he knew it was gone – despite his futile hope that he'd be able to overcompensate for his blindness.

Rose wanted to be strong for her love, but still didn't know yet how to react to show that strength. Her silence, though, did the speaking. Whereas Rose had seen her passionate husband tear up several times before, she had never seen him collapse into the hopelessness of full-on crying. Until now.

"It's gone, Rose. It's all gone," he said through the fit of tears streaming down his face. "It's gone, Rose." Was all that he could repeat.

Instinctively, she held him in her arms. She caressed the tears from off his cheeks while running her fingers through his hair.

"It's all gone," he again blurted out through his despair.

"I know, Ethan." She tried to reassure him, not even sure that her words were heard through his sobbing. She tried to get him talking, hoping that conversation about it might somehow calm him down.

"When did it leave, Ethan?"

He sniffled, trying to compose himself enough to answer her question. "I saw it slowly leave while painting you for the last hour." He wiped some more tears off of his cheek. "I really thought I could finish for you. But it's gone, Rose."

She held him in her arms, overcome by the sadness her husband was feeling.

"Ethan, it'll be okay. I promise. I still love you. I'll *always* love you."

Rose felt Ethan try to compose himself again. He stopped crying before kissing her on the forehead. "I know. I love you too."

But Rose wasn't going to let it end there. What had been an evening of warmth and electricity between them was not ending with Ethan feeling as though he had to compromise his emotions.

While they held each other in their arms, Rose looked him right in the eyes. "I mean it, Ethan. You're my everything…"

"I know," Ethan said again. But Rose quickly brushed that aside. She took her hand and held his face in it. She continued to stare into his eyes. Even though she knew Ethan couldn't see her back, she'd hoped that the shadowy outline of herself would tell him that she meant every word she was about to say next.

"No, listen to me. Ethan – from the moment I met you, I loved you. And as the years have passed by, I've seen it. There's something about you, Ethan. You have such a gift for seeing beauty. But not just seeing it, *feeling* it, and appreciating it. Your whole life you have chased what it is that can make something beautiful – something purposeful and meaningful. You've sought to share that with other people through your art and any other way that you could. While you've lost your sight, you've opened mine. I see life differently now because of you."

She lovingly gripped his face a little tighter, letting him know that she was serious. "And, Ethan, it's because the whole time beauty wasn't around you – it was *in* you. *You* are beautiful, in every possible way imaginable. Every way. We all see it. It's not just because of your ability to paint. It's in you. You'll learn to express it in different ways over time. And through it all, I will be right next to you. Not because you deserve it. And not because I'm supposed to be. But because I *want* to. I choose you, Ethan."

Many of the tears they'd shed since Ethan had broken the news of his blindness had been tears of sadness. But by the time that Rose now finished pouring her heart out to him, they both were embraced by tears that were shed in happiness. Ethan had never before had someone speak right to his core as Rose did just now. No one got him more than Rose – not even himself.

Ethan smiled and kissed her on the lips, letting the blissful feeling between them be taken into their souls.

"Thank you," he whispered once their lips departed.

"Come on," she said. "We should get going home before our babysitter decides she'll never sit for us again." Just as always, Rose found the perfect quip to lighten the moment.

They held hands as they left his studio and locked up the entire gallery for the evening.

"What should we do with my portrait of you?" He asked on the walk back to their car in the cool evening breeze.

"Well, I mean – it could definitely give Picasso a run for his money."

"You think so?"

"Yeah ... maybe not. I could at least tell that you were trying to paint a person. Picasso's ... not so much."

Rose's joke made Ethan chuckle probably more than it should have. But then Rose asked the question that had been on her mind since she'd seen his unfortunate attempt at painting her.

"Ethan, does this mean that you might forget what I look like? … you know, since the portrait didn't…"

But she wasn't able to finish her question before Ethan quickly interjected. "No, absolutely not."

"But I thought that's why you were painting them. So, why not?"

"Don't worry at all about that. Trust me."

They both opened their car doors, and the rest of the short ride home remained silent. Rose did trust him. And for that reason, she didn't question him any further. But still, her mind drifted toward what Ethan meant. It was as if there was something she was missing – a final puzzle piece to a puzzle that she didn't even know existed. On the drive home, she couldn't stop thinking about how Ethan's response was mysterious, but it wasn't the first time tonight she got that feeling. The other times were when he tried to cover up the existence of another painting which she hadn't known about. Something was up, and Rose knew it.

Chapter 22

That same night, a loud bump from outside their master bedroom awoke Rose. She instantly sat up, worried that one of their children had stumbled out of bed. Or worse yet – an intruder might be in their upscale house.

"Ethan," she whispered. But when she put her hand on his side of the bed to wake him up, she knew what was really going on. Ethan was not lying next to her, which meant that he was stumbling around blindly in their dark house.

But why, Rose wondered. With the air of mystery still fresh from their car ride home, something felt off to her about what was going on. For that reason, she quietly opened her bedroom door and tiptoed through the house searching for Ethan.

The house was dark in the middle of the night, but she saw a dim light shining from a crack in the door leading to their study. She slowly cracked the door open to see what Ethan was doing in his study so late. She was relieved that the door did not make a sound as it became ajar, giving her an uninterrupted view of her husband on the other side.

Rose expected to find him reflectively going through his desk, maybe putting things away in boxes to start a new chapter in his life. But that was far from what she saw.

She stood surprised, watching her husband, not understanding the scene which she had stumbled upon so unexpectedly.

Ethan stood in front of a painting they had purchased so many years ago. It was the painting that she was so adamant about owning, so they'd bought it and brought it home. From the moment she saw it, it's depth and emotion instantly pulled her in – not just because it was a painting of a rose, but because of how it was painted. There was such passion in the pedals, and she had felt that same emotion every time she would see it since. Beauty radiated from its brush strokes – but not just in its light - from its shadows as well. And now, Ethan stood in the shadows holding his fingers up to it.

Rose watched as her blind husband traced the contours of the brushstrokes. In the dim light of the study, she saw his blind eyes staring straight down as if the lines of the painting were bringing back a memory which he was able to visualize in his mind. A quick smile crossed his mind as he traced the outline of one pedal, captivated in his mind by what it made him think.

Rose now knew that intimacy of this silent, intense moment to Ethan was the final puzzle piece she wondered about on the ride home. She just didn't know what it meant.

She was hesitant to interrupt his personal moment, but she had to know. She had to know what her husband was thinking – where his mind had traveled to now that he could not be captivated by the visual beauty of the painting.

"Ethan," she said softly, trying not to startle him.

He wasn't startled, rather he looked up and smiled – almost as if he expected her to find him at some point.

"Ethan, what do you see?" Such a poignant question. And Ethan had always been the one to ask it to others. But for the first time, he was now being asked it.

"I see you," he said – a sincere smile radiating from his face.

"What do you mean?" She inquired. Like a student wanting to learn from a professor, Rose was inquisitive and wanting to have her husband's perspective poured on her.

"Come here for a moment, Rose," he said, now holding his hand out for her to grab it.

She came close and put her hand into his. He then moved

her hand up to the painting so that her fingers brushed the texture of the rose. He moved his fingers to her eyes and closed them.

"Rose," he said softly. "Rose – I painted this the night I met you."

The weight of his words soaked into her very being, and she couldn't help but begin tearing up at the lovely shock he divulged to her. In surprise, she glanced at him. But when seeing the sincere look on his face, she looked back at the painting and knew why she had always felt emotionally intertwined with its beauty. The rose was her.

"It's beautiful," she confessed. She had said this many times in the past when describing the painting. But this time, the words carried even more meaning. She wanted to ask question after question, but something inside of her told her to just feel the moment, and Ethan would say what he needed to say.

She closed her eyes with her fingers on the painting, and just felt the paint. It made sense now. The thick painting and heavy brushstrokes were the same as the portraits he'd painted of their children. He could feel this painting just as he could the others. So, now – in the peaceful still of the night, Rose did what her husband had done countless times. She traced the contours of the painting to really feel its beauty. Appreciation is the closest word to convey how she felt in that moment, but even that word fell short. For, some emotions are unable to be captured by words.

The feeling was magnified by Ethan's soft explanation. "Rose, I will never, ever forget what you look like. I can't. Just as the beauty of a rose is undeniable, so too is your inner beauty that radiates and is portrayed on your face and through your movements. It's as though your very existence is the greatest work of art I ever had the gift of setting my eyes on.

Any time I grew frustrated with losing my sight, all I had to do was come trace my greatest painting ever. I painted this the night I met you. It burst out of me as if fate was holding the paintbrush. I'd never painted an impressionist painting before, and I never have since. This painting isn't me, it's you. And any time I need reminded that everything will be okay, I come trace this painting to remind me."

Rose still held her fingers up to the painting, but now they were trembling at the beautiful words being spoken to her from the man she'd loved since the night she met him. She trembled in humility, for that is what the magnificence of beauty can create in a person. Ethan's words wrapped her in a warmth beyond any feeling she had experienced before, and she stood humbled by the warmth which she'd felt so grateful to have been embraced by.

"Rose, I trace it to remind me that – for as magnificently beautiful as this rose is, the beauty of my Rose transcends even this. Your beauty cannot be captured in a painting, and that helps me remember what you look like. Just as I remember painting each of these brushstrokes on this rose, I remember each brushstroke of you because you far surpass this painting.

And it brings me peace and hope to know that such beauty exists in this world which can't even be captured on canvas. I was so scared for so long about losing my eyesight. I thought the scariest part was letting go – but I was wrong. By letting go of what I could see, I can hold onto what matters most to me. And that's you, Rose. It's you, and it's always been you. I don't know what the future holds. But I have you. And together I know we can face anything.

You're the most beautiful creation I have ever witnessed. And knowing that I have such beauty in my life fills me with hope. You're my hope, Rose. I love you."

Rose looked at the man who, earlier that evening, she had

admired in a similar, passionately appreciative way. She took her hand off of the painting and caressed his face. Closing her eyes, she traced the contours of his features as though it was a painting, grateful to have found such a beautiful creation in her life.

She then leaned in and kissed Ethan. Ethan leaned in and kissed her back. And in this moment, the two most beautiful works of art existed as one.

The End.

Your Review on Amazon is Greatly Appreciated.

<u>Social Media</u>:
Facebook.com/AuthorKyleShoop
Instagram.com/WriterKyle
Twitter.com/WriterKyle
www.KyleShoop.com

Join the Newsletter for Info on Future Books, by emailing kyleshoop@gmail.com or visit kyleshoop.com

(Turn the page for a preview of Book #3 in this series.)

A special preview of Book Three from
The "Senses of Love" Series:

A Taste of Love

By

Kyle Shoop

Available Mid-2020

Chapter 1

There are really only a handful of moments in life which could be considered truly defining. The birth of a child. The loss of a loved one. Your wedding day. A first kiss. A first job. A job loss – or even a job change to avoid the ritualistic pattern of daily life. Out of all of the time in life spent searching for meaningful moments, really there may only be a handful of actual defining moments.

But Nikki wasn't searching for a defining moment. Instead, she was searching for a fulfilling one. One of those incredibly unique moments where it makes all of life – the hard moments and the mundane ones – completely and unequivocally worth it. Nikki was searching for that rare moment where she discovered love. Or, rather – that moment where love discovered her. She knew that once she found the type of unequivocal love which she was looking for, that she'd want nothing more to hold onto it for the rest of her life. So, simply put, she wasn't just searching love, she was also searching for her future husband.

To say that Nikki sought out love would be correct, but not totally accurate as to her approach. She wasn't just seeking out love, she actually being so bold as to be interviewing for it. And since she knew that she'd eventually marry love when she found him, this also meant that Nikki's quest for love also resulted in her actively interviewing to find her future husband. Her interviews for a husband wasn't her goal – that was the byproduct of what she really wanted in life: love.

Nikki knew that her lifetime of love existed in the world somewhere. And until she found it, she made the decision to actively be engaged to discover it. She figured that she had to – the whole world was full of candidates. So, if she was going to find him, she had to get going!

To Nikki, her faith that she would eventually find love never wavered. She knew it was just a matter of numbers. Love was somewhere out in the world – and she hoped that it happened to be in her backyard of New York City.

Nikki always just knew that she'd recognize her future husband – the love of her life – almost immediately upon meeting him. And she knew that he'd recognize her back as his equal. It wasn't really a pie-in-the-sky or knight-in-shining-armor dream for Nikki, either. If she remained single for the rest of her life, that was fine. She knew that she would have given it the best shot she could, and that was good enough for her. But since she didn't prefer it that way, Nikki took action. It was a modern woman approach, for sure.

And there was definitely a basis for Nikki believing that

she'd eventually find love. She'd had several friends over the years who would appear single one week, and then suddenly engaged the next. Just like that. And when Nikki asked them each how that happened, each of her girl friends would similarly remark how they just suddenly met him and knew. So, this type of sudden love existed – both to those other girls, as well as in Nikki's mind.

So, to Nikki, it was also going to happen to her. Why wouldn't it? After all, she was an attractive, accomplished blonde woman in her early thirties living in the largest city in the nation. She maintained a schedule of working, going to the gym, seeing friends and family, getting out into the city, and … interviewing for her future husband.

Nikki's interviews in her search for love occurred via dates which normally occurred twice every week. The first date was mid-week every Wednesday evening. The second date was every Saturday evening. If the Wednesday date went well, then she would invite the guy for a second date that same Saturday. However, that was just her plan - so far, it had never happened. Since she began this schedule for first dates, no guy had ever actually advanced to the second date. Not yet. Nikki was picky and didn't want to give a guy a second date just for any reason. Again, she'd know love when she met him.

But it wasn't just the schedule which she maintained on a strictly consistent basis. She was also was extremely consistent with the location and time of her first dates. Each date was exactly the same and began with a dinner date. She would meet each guy at 7:00 p.m. at Fate's Kitchen in Manhattan. The restaurant was named after its owner and chef, Joey Fate. And although Nikki had gotten to know Joey well over the last several years, she still preferred this modern, sit-down restaurant for its name. She was hoping that meeting at Fate's Kitchen would help fate itself to intervene.

Of course, if a second date happened with a guy, then Nikki would have to plan to go somewhere else. Ironically, down the street from Fate's Kitchen was an off-Broadway theatre named Second Chance Theatre. Due to its name, she obviously kept that in the back of her mind for if a second date was to happen. But that would be a bridge to cross when it happened. And as to meeting so early in the evening at 7:00 p.m., that was also intentional. If the date wasn't going well, then she could always use a fictious previously-planned engagement to end the date early. She had it all planned.

But incredibly, she took this strict routine about her first dates even a step farther.

During her dates, she would ask the exact same questions. She'd often make the same exact off-handed jokes as well. This was done with well-rehearsed precision so as not to give away the fact that she was actually interviewing each candidate. The purpose behind this act was simple: to better compare each guy to each other. By eliminating as many variances on her part from the dates as she could, she was able to see each guy's personality traits and tendencies more clearly. She figured this would help her know love more easily when it manifested. She wasn't sure if it would come from one guy being unique from the others, or if it would be depicted in his sincere interest in her being reciprocated. But, Nikki figured that having this routine was beneficial. Or, maybe, she was just so actively looking for love that she didn't want to have to plan so many different dates out. That was possible, too. Either way, it was her plan – and a well-rehearsed one at that.

Of course, she sought to shroud her interview technique in a veil of light-hearted conversation. She had to - to try and make her interviews look off-handed and unrehearsed. It was, after all, still a date where she was searching for love instead of merely filling the position of a husband.

If she had wanted just a husband, Nikki knew that she could easily have found that by now. There were enough men on both ends of the social spectrum – from desperate to conceded – who would pick up the first attractive and willing blonde that they could find in life. This was New York City, after all – a concrete jungle of intentions. No, Nikki wanted more. Love was her lofty goal, and she knew it took work. Again, to her, it was a numbers game. It would happen – eventually.

A Taste of Love

Her dating technique naturally required precision and experience. By now, this was a well-rehearsed performance to Nikki. She'd become a pro at reading each different situation and speaking with energy and engagement to make it sound as though she had not been through the process countless times before. And by the end of her first summer doing this, Nikki had enough experience to read each situation, each date, and each guy like a well-studied play. So much so, that she could often predict how the date would end. And it never ended with a second date – for a multitude of differing reasons.

Finding new guys to take on dates was never an issue. After all, New York City was the largest city in the nation. It was an endless well of candidates. She'd found setting up dates extremely easy, too. In this day and age, men often welcomed a woman stepping up to show initiative to ask him out – especially a spunky, personable, caring, and attractive woman. And Nikki checked each of those boxes.

The field of candidates was scheduled from a multitude of sources. Dating apps were no doubt prevalent, but she didn't stick to just those due to men on them often having intentions which were not conducive of really finding love. And those intentions of the men from dating apps were not among the traits that would make Nikki want a second date with them. Instead, she'd also meet guys at the gym, through friends or family, and just generally from being out and about in the city.

But most frequently, she'd meet guys through her work.

Oh, they weren't co-workers. Rather, Nikki worked in catering – a field dominated by women. She'd received her culinary arts degree with her sights set on opening her own kitchen. But not just any kitchen – one focused on specialty pastries and desserts. Even though Nikki truly believed she would encounter love by happenstance with hard work, she had the opposite opinion of actually opening her own specialty dessert business. She just didn't think it would ever happen. Opening her own business was too impractical, especially for having chosen to live in the most expensive city in the nation.

So instead, she took a well-paying job in catering. She figured that it was at least related to her real interest. And it even got her close to her dream. She'd constantly help cater and serve at a wide range of events from reunions, work parties, corporate functions, and bah mitzvahs. But her absolute favorite thing were weddings. Hands down.

It wasn't just that weddings were full of men who she'd easily stare down to schedule into her weekly interviews. And it also wasn't that weddings radiated love, and Nikki sought that like a desired treasure. Rather, weddings were Nikki's favorite part of her job because of the one thing that was always at each one: the wedding cake.

Sometimes wedding guests would catch her staring at the cakes. Many times, this resulted in the bride feeling complimented about the cake, having incorrectly assumed that Nikki was gawking at how fabulously it was done. Nope. That's not what Nikki was staring at. Rather, she was staring because it was her dream to be hired as the chef for the cake instead of being stuck in the remedial position of server and caterer. And she knew that she could match – if not exceed – the way in which each of the cakes looked.

Unfortunately, Nikki's employer was never hired for the pastries, and especially not for the wedding cake. Nikki had once tried to approach her boss to allow her to start a cake-making service to include within the catering business. But he declined. Apparently, Nikki was too valuable in what she already did for her to branch her time out elsewhere.

Once, at a wedding, Nikki had overheard a bride tell her guest how much she had paid for her wedding cake. It left Nikki speechless. It was a significant amount, which Nikki assumed was because weddings in New York City were big businesses. This gave Nikki fuel to her dream of one day opening her own pastry business. And this was even more fuel compared to the confidence that Nikki already had in knowing that she could easily make the wide range of decorated cakes that she'd been caught staring at. But still, she had bills. Real life responsibility. And those all kept her from taking the leap to start her own company.

So, Nikki had two goals in live: to find love, and to

actually become a pastry chef. To her, though, one of those goals was realistic, while the other was unattainable. Luckily, she figured that love was the realistic goal. This was because if she had to choose between those two goals, she easily chose love. That was why Nikki kept her routine of interviewing to find it – she knew it would happen eventually.

Being Wednesday evening, Nikki entered Fate's Kitchen and waited at her usual table. She knew the owner from having catered his son's graduation party, so she had the fix for her twice-weekly table in the happening restaurant.

And just like every other time, Nikki arrive about twenty minutes early. She also did this on purpose. Just as an interviewee who was truly interested in a position would arrive a little early, Nikki did the same thing for her dates. Only, her early arrival was to actually see if the guy was so interested that he'd be early. And sometimes, they were early. That always checked a box for Nikki and gave the guy a head-start at showing his potential.

But not tonight. As the minutes approached 7:00 pm, it became clear that this guy wasn't going to be arriving early. That never rubbed Nikki wrong, though. She always wanted to be open to each guy being the one, so she did everything she could to give each man his fair chance. Tonight was no different.

No matter how many times she'd done it before, one thing always remained the same. Nikki's anticipation was through the roof. She really did want to find love – and, for all she knew, tonight could be the night.

Her heart skipped a beat when she saw the man approach her table. He was as cute. Extending his hand to shake hers, the man introduced himself.

"Hi Nicole, I'm Lucas."

End Chapter 1

Full Book Available 2020

To receive release date information for all books in this series, sign up for the author newsletter by emailing KyleShoop@gmail.com, or by visiting www.KyleShoop.com

The first book in this series, *The Sound of Love*, is already released.

ABOUT THE AUTHOR

Kyle Shoop is the author of novels in several genres. This book, *The Sight of Love*, is the second book in his romance "Senses of Love" series. There are planned to be five books in this series. His prior series is the *Acea Bishop Trilogy*. It is a fantasy-adventure trilogy, and all three books are now available in E-book and paperback. The first book is entitled *Acea and the Animal Kingdom*.

Kyle lives in Utah with his wife and children. Kyle was recognized at a young age for his storytelling by being awarded the first-place Gold Key award for fiction writing in Washington State. Since then, Kyle's inspiration for writing has been to create and share compelling stories, regardless of the genre.

For more information on Kyle's books, and to sign up for his author newsletter which announces new books, please visit:

www.KyleShoop.com
Facebook.com/AuthorKyleShoop
Instagram.com/WriterKyle
Twitter.com/WriterKyle

Made in the USA
Middletown, DE
12 July 2021